HIS PET

WARLORD'S CAPTIVE DUET
BOOK TWO

SINISTRE ANGE

GTB PUBLISHING

GTB PUBLISHING

Cover by Covers by Sophie

ISBN: 978-1964736-112

1

Bella wriggled her way out from underneath Alex's arm. He groaned and made a sleepy, protesting noise, but allowed her to go. Since he'd pretty much exhausted himself in the pool, and then inside of her, she wasn't surprised that he was tired. But she was feeling energized and strangely hopeful.

There were four of the sigils in the room that denoted where a secret passageway was. She doubted that the one next to the main door opened since that would be pointless. But that still left three options. The only question was: was anyone watching?

Since the night they'd had their sexual exploits while she'd been under the influence of the aphrodisiac spread across a screen for the Wolf's soldiers' entertainment, she and Alex had basically been operating under the assumption that someone could be watching at any time. But there had been no indication that anyone had since then. Maybe the cameras had only been activated because they'd wanted to see what Alex would do when she came back to the room horny and begging.

After all, it wasn't like any of their activities with the Wolf had been put up for public consumption. So maybe the cameras weren't always on. Maybe she and Alex were being too paranoid. It seemed like wishful thinking, but maybe there was a way she could test it.

Looking up at the ceiling, she noted that in the corners of the room and the angles where the walls met the ceiling, she couldn't see anything that looked like a camera. So if they were there, they were behind the walls. Thinking that over, Bella cleaned up the cum that was starting to leak out of her with a corner of the sheet, blushing as she thought about what she and Alex had just done. She didn't regret it. At all. But would he?

They never talked about what they would do when the Wolf let them go. Or if they did somehow manage to escape first. At least, they didn't talk about whatever this was between them.

Not that Bella wanted to have that conversation yet. How could they know how they would feel once they were out of captivity? She didn't think her feelings for Alex were going to go away, but she didn't know if he felt the same. And it seemed kind of unfair to push that on him while they were trapped together. Better to say nothing at all for now.

Looking back up at the ceiling, Bella waved her arms above her head. "Hey! I'm hungry! Can we get some food in here?"

Alex's groan as he woke distracted her and she turned to see him blearily staring at her from the center of the bed, the sheets rumpled around him. Sexy, but obviously exhausted.

"What are you doing?" he asked with a sleepy groan. The normalcy of his tone made her smile.

"Trying to get some food," she answered, turning back around and waving her arms again.

She wasn't really that hungry. If someone actually brought food, she would eat, but mostly she just wanted to know if there would be a response. Alex groaned again and she heard the soft thump as he fell back into place on the bed. Deciding not to disturb his rest anymore, Bella sat down at the table, staring at the door.

And waited.

And waited.

And waited.

She started singing in her head to pass the time.

Nothing.

She looked back up at the sigil on the wall, not five feet away from her. Standing up, she went over to it and traced her fingers along the S-curve, almost absently. Not following the pattern Trish had given her, just to see if someone would come in and stop her. A loud snore from the bed made her jump a bit, but nothing else happened.

Holding her breath, she pressed as she'd been directed. The right end of the bar, the left end, the bottom curve, the top curve, and then three fingers on where the S intersected.

Nothing.

Bella did it again just to be sure. More nothing. But Trish had said that not all of them led to passageways. Or at least that's what Jordan had told supposedly her and it did make sense.

There was another one over the bed, but Bella didn't think that very likely, so she turned to the wall where the television screen had been. Now that one might make more sense. Walking over, she dragged her fingers along the surface as she did so, although she was feeling more confident by the minute that she was unobserved, that the Wolf had only taped them because he'd known there'd be something to watch.

Today, though, when everyone was distracted by whatever mission they were on, and Alex and Bella were just afterthoughts? Why bother?

Reaching the sigil, she ran her fingers along it, waiting. Still a bit cautious. Just in case. She couldn't help but listen for the door to open and soldiers to come bursting through.

Nothing. Again.

She pressed her fingers against the sigil, harder this time. The right end of the bar, the left end, the bottom curve, the top curve, and then three fingers on where the S intersected.

And to her left, a hole opened up. Bella gasped in shock. Even though Trish had told her, some part of her hadn't quite believed, had thought that maybe it was a trick.

But there it was.

Stepping to her left, she faced it square on, looking down the long, narrow hall. The light was dim but there was enough for visibility while walking. Bella turned back to look at the bed.

"Alex? Alex?"

No response. He was still out of it. Should she wake him? He'd want to know, but then again, she'd rather only get herself into trouble, just in case she did get caught. And if she woke him up, who knew what his reaction might be. If he'd even be able to think straight. He was exhausted.

The opening slid shut, automatically, while she was

still standing there staring at it. If she went into the passageway, she'd be able to get out the same way. That's what Trish had said. And also that Jordan had warned her the passageways were complex and it was easy to get lost, especially since there were no markers to indicate where you were once you were in them.

Bella opened the door again and stared at it, trying to gather her courage. Eventually it closed and she still hadn't stepped into it.

Okay. This was stupid. If someone was watching, they would have come to stop her by now. Wouldn't they have? It couldn't hurt to at least go inside and look around. She could head in one direction only and keep track by counting the sigils she passed. That made the most sense.

This time, when she opened the passageway, she stepped into it and stood there until the door closed behind her. Letting out a long breath, she looked in the three directions she could go; left, right, or straight ahead. Going straight ahead seemed smartest, that way as long as she didn't make any turns, she could just come straight back.

Walking forward, she couldn't help the tingling inside of her chest, of both anxiety and excitement. The giddy feeling that came from knowing she was doing something dangerous, the exhilaration that came from being fairly certain she wasn't going to be caught. She'd only walked about thirty paces when she came to the next sigil, on the right side of the wall. Pressing her ear against it, she could hear voices; loud enough to be audible, but not quite loud enough to be distinct. She couldn't hear what they were saying, but at least it was a warning that people were there. Trying that with the next two sigils she came to, she could hear people behind the second one but not the third.

She almost opened up that one, just to see what was there, but caution stayed her hand. What if there were soldiers there who were just being quiet? The idea made her too nervous. Maybe the passageways weren't quite as useful as she'd thought they would be, not without actually knowing where each of them led to.

Up ahead was an intersection, and she picked up the pace a little bit, wanting to know if she might see some kind of marker or directional indicator that Trish had missed. After all, Bella had a lot more time to look around than Trish had—at least that was what she assumed, considering how Jordan dragged the young blonde around at his long-legged pace.

When she got to the intersection she glanced right and then left... and froze.

Fear and shock weakened her knees and her legs gave out beneath her, leaving her kneeling and leaning forward on her hands as shivering tremors shook her body.

Jordan shook his head at her, his arms crossed over his chest. Two soldiers she didn't recognize stood behind him. By his side was Trish, kneeling on the ground, a red ball gag in her mouth and a pleading expression on her face. She stared straight at Bella, looking agonized. For one sharp moment, Bella wondered if Trish had betrayed her... but Jordan's next words cut through that theory.

He rested his hand on top of Trish's head, stroking it back and making the young woman shudder. "What bad girls you two are," he said, his deep voice laced with a kind of satisfaction. He wrapped his fingers around

Trish's hair and used it to haul her to her feet. Jerking his head at Bella, he looked over his shoulder at the two soldiers. "Bring her."

Bella couldn't do anything but stare in horror, a small voice in the back of her brain cursing her own misguided confidence as the soldiers approached.

2

Warmth receded as his sheets were yanked back and Alex came slamming back into consciousness with a yell, lashing out and automatically trying to fight as hard hands grasped his wrists. Even though the sleep hadn't cleared from his eyes yet, he managed to land at least one good punch before pain shuddered through his body, fizzing along his nerves and he went crashing back down onto the bed.

At least it was a soft landing.

He groaned, a strangled sound, which was the only noise his vocal cords seemed capable of while the electricity moved through him.

It stopped as suddenly as it had started, leaving him shaking. Dazed, this time he didn't resist as he was dragged from the bed. His feet stumbled on the ground before he found footing, soldiers on either side of him gripping his arms to keep him from falling completely. Their rough grips hurt his sensitive skin that was still tingling from the electric shock. Not that he said anything.

"So who put money on him getting one of us?" one of the soldiers asked, making Alex look up, trying to get a handle on what was happening.

One of the other soldiers was rubbing his cheek, which was showing a distinct dark-red mark on it, but he grinned. "I did. Worth every penny."

The others groaned, their good-natured ribbing flowing around Alex, pricking at his temper. It gave him a rush of adrenaline that helped kick his brain back into gear. He craned his neck around.

"Where's Bella?"

The soldier that he'd hit smirked at him. "She's indisposed. And you're being moved for now."

Before he had a chance to ask any more questions, they'd stopped and one of the soldiers put his hand on a panel next to the door. Alex was shoved into the room, the door whisking shut behind him. It had a couch, a bookshelf that was filled with books, a table and two chairs, but was otherwise completely sterile. There was something different about it though, something that Alex couldn't quite put his finger on. And it wasn't just the bookshelf—although that was a welcome sight.

He looked around the room, trying to figure out what was niggling at the back of his mind, frowning as he examined every inch of the space.

It wasn't until he sat down on the couch and all the hairs on the back of his neck lifted as he stared at the wall in front of him that he figured it out. The walls were completely bare, without a single decoration... not even one sigil.

He surged to his feet, buoyed up by pure adrenaline and fear for Bella. What the hell had she done?

Stupid. Stupid, stupid, stupid.

Even though she'd just wanted to see what was inside and hadn't actually been planning on going anywhere, exploring had been monumentally stupid. Although at the time she'd felt secure and she'd done everything she could make sure she wasn't being watched. She still wasn't entirely sure if Jordan had already known she was in there or if he'd just happened to be in the tunnels at the same time.

They went through the passageway until he opened up a room that she'd never seen before, although she recognized quite a bit of the equipment in it. This was obviously the room below the Wolf's main hall, the one that came up through the floor. That or it was an exact replica, because it had the same bed and wooden structures that they'd seen up on the dais. But down here there were all sorts of things lining the walls, things that Bella didn't even want to look at.

Jordan had Bella's hands cuffed together in front of her before forcing her to kneel a few feet away from him and Trish. The other soldiers lounged in the doorway, watching, although obviously not expecting to be invited any further into the room. Bella doubted they seriously thought she was that much of an escape threat right now, even if it was obvious that Jordan's attention was almost completely focused on Trish.

The pretty blonde was trussed up, her wrist cuffs attached to a hook that stretched her out. Ankle cuffs kept her legs spread apart, just wide enough for her to balance but making all the soft, sensitive areas between her legs completely vulnerable. Her wide blue eyes were trained on Jordan as he moved around the room; she didn't once glance at Bella. The ball-gag didn't allow her to make much noise, but Bella was sure she could hear little whimpers anyway.

Coming back in front of Trish, Jordan cupped one of her breasts in his big hands. Her head tipped back as she looked up at him, wide-eyed and shaking, even though Bella could tell that his touch was actually quite gentle. The scene in front of her seemed almost intimate, and she wanted to look away, but she couldn't. There was something very different about the way Jordan treated Trish and the way the Wolf treated her and Alex, and this was her first chance to really see it up close. She was fascinated.

Trish's long blonde hair hung down her back, slightly tangled and mussed-looking, swaying gently as she shook her head while Jordan squeezed and kneaded her breasts. His hands were so big on her small frame that he was able to completely engulf the mounds with his palms. Even though she was obviously scared, Bella could tell that Trish was also becoming aroused. The way her back arched, despite the limited movement allowed by her position, pressed her breasts further into Jordan's hands.

And when he moved away, Trish shuddered and whimpered.

Even though she didn't want to be, Bella was becoming aroused herself from watching them. It was a strange symphony of reluctance on Trish's part, obsessive desire on Jordan's, and the amalgamation of punishment and gentle tenderness that stirred something within Bella. She'd already learned that she could be sexually excited by things that she didn't think she should be, but she hadn't realized that it would extend to this kind of voyeurism. Pressing her thighs together, Bella shivered as she watched Jordan pinch and tug on Trish's nipples. His head was lowered; it looked like he was whispering in her ear. Bella desperately wished she could hear what he was saying.

Once Trish's nipples were fully extended, hard and pointy, Jordan straightened and reached into his pocket, pulling out what Bella immediately recognized as a set of nipple clamps. She whimpered in sympathy as Jordan closed a clamp over one of Trish's nipples. Trish's entire body shuddered, but she didn't pull away... she just closed her eyes and held as still as possible, her chest moving as she breathed in deeply through the pain, and Bella realized that this was definitely not Trish's first time with the clamps. Jordan clamped her other nipple, leaving the chain connecting the two hanging between her breasts, and then he stroked her sides, watching her reaction, his fingers moving up and down the curve of her body, almost as if he was soothing her, even though he was the one who had caused her pain.

There was a strange fluttering in her stomach, and Bella was shocked when she realized that she was actually envious. After all, no one had soothed or helped her when she'd been clamped or punished; she'd had no kind of encouragement at all. Not even Alex had been allowed to comfort her. But Jordan was doing so with Trish.

Once Trish seemed to have adjusted to the clamps, Jordan walked around behind her to pick up a long, flat leather paddle. He glanced over to where the soldiers were still in the doorway, silently standing at attention and watching. Bella bit her lower lip, even though they weren't watching her. When Jordan walked around behind the trussed-up blonde, drawing his arm back and landing the first blow across her ass, Bella realized that Trish had been positioned so that her breasts would thrust out at the soldiers as her body arched in reaction to the blow. As if Jordan was almost deliberately taunting them with what he had and they didn't... or maybe just showing her off. Similar to the way the Wolf seemed to enjoy showing off Alex and Bella.

Was everyone here either an exhibitionist or a voyeur?

THWACK!

A second blow across Trish's bottom had the young blonde shrieking into her gag and Bella wincing in sympathy. She had the urge to speak up, to beg Jordan to stop because Trish couldn't, but a craven voice in her head whispered to be silent lest his attention turn to her. Right now she was almost forgotten... but she doubted she would remain that way for long if she tried to interfere.

THWACK! THWACK!

The sound of leather slapping against tender skin made Bella jerk with every blow, just as Trish did. Bella's hands clenched into fists, almost as if she was physically restraining herself from crying out along with the other woman, her body trembling in reaction to what she was watching.

After five hefty smacks against Trish's ass, which had to be bright red by now, Jordan stopped. Holding the paddle at his side, he stepped up closer behind Trish again, winding his hand in her hair, looping it around his fingers under his hand was just at the nape of her neck and then he used it to bend her head back. Bella could hear the soft murmur of his voice as he whispered in

Trish's ear although she still couldn't hear what he was saying. The other woman whimpered.

And then Jordan stepped back again.

THWACK!

THWACK!

The distressed sounds Trish was making behind her gag made Bella want to cover her ears, but the space between the cuffs on her wrists was too small for her to be able to cover both. Closing her eyes didn't help at all. It was like the scene was burned into her brain: Trish's agonized, muffled sounds, the jingling of the chain between her nipples as her body jerked and bounced, and the slap of the paddle.

THWACK!

"Stop! Please..." Bella shouted out the first word, the second came as more of a whimper, trickling off as she opened her eyes to see Jordan's icy gaze sweeping over to her. He raised his eyebrow.

"Feeling guilty, Pet?" he asked, his lips curving upward. "Would you like to help her?"

Bella's voice felt like it was caught in her throat, behind an invisible barrier. What had she done? But she did want to help Trish, so she nodded her head.

Jordan smirked.

Stroking his hand down Trish's side, he turned his arm to curve his hand over her mound and dip his fingers into her pussy. They came away wet. Lifting his hand, he showed his glistening fingers to Bella, simultaneously showing the other soldiers, who murmured their appreciation. "When she comes, her punishment ends."

Trish made a noise behind the gag, but there was no way to tell what she was trying to say or express. Stepping closer to Bella, Jordan dragged his fingers over her lips, leaving her with no doubt as to how he thought Trish would achieve orgasm.

It was her fault Trish was in this position in the first place. Trish had been trying to do something good, something helpful for her and Alex, and Bella had gone and fucked it all up. And now Trish was paying the price.

So when Jordan turned away and stepped back toward Trish, tapping the leather paddle meaningfully against his leg, Bella followed as best she could on all fours with her wrists cuffed together. But when Jordan moved behind Trish, Bella went in front until she was kneeling almost between Trish's legs. Behind her she could hear the soldiers at the door laughing, probably settling some kind of bet. Assholes. Why the Wolf's men had such a fascination with her and Alex's behavior and reactions, she would never understand.

Despite the fact that Trish was in obvious pain from the leather paddle, from this close Bella could smell the musky scent of her arousal and see Trish's slick netherlips up close. Jordan really hadn't had to work hard to find the cream to coat his fingers. Strangely, what Bella mostly felt was a sense of relief to know that she wasn't the only one who had inexplicable reactions like this.

THWACK!

The blow jolted Trish's hips forward and the younger woman screamed behind her gag, her chest heaving as she struggled with the sensations.

And the best thing Bella could do for her, the only way she could help, was to tilt her head back and lean forward to bury her mouth in Trish's splayed pussy. She felt Trish shudder above her as Bella swiped her tongue up the center of Trish's lips. Musky sweetness, tinged with just the slightest hint of bitter, exploded in her mouth; the distinct taste of pussy that wasn't quite like anything else.

She felt the next blow to Trish's ass, pushing Trish's pussy even more firmly against her mouth. Bella was gentle, wary of her teeth bruising those soft lips while Trish's movements were so unpredictable. Especially once Trish started to press her pussy against Bella's questing tongue, trying to escape her punishment and replace it with pleasure.

They both sagged with relief when the steady paddling stopped again. Bella had winced every time the paddle had smacked against Trish's cheeks, not just because of Trish's jerking movement, but also because it felt dangerously close to her face even though she was protected by Trish's body.

Something brushed against her chin and, when she glanced, she saw Jordan's fingers pushing into Trish's ass. The other woman mewled piteously behind her gag, wriggling and obviously unhappy with this turn of events. Bella could sympathize. Especially as Jordan slid his fingers from Trish's ass and replaced them with his cock.

Bella shuddered as she felt Trish's reaction, the way her body surged forward, away from the punishing thrust. Her muffled cry of protest was overpowered by Jordan's groan of pleasure. Behind her she could hear the answering groans from the soldiers in the doorway, and she could only speculate how the entire tableau must look to them, with Bella kneeling before Trish, her face buried in Trish's muff, the slender blonde caught between her and Jordan as he reached up to cup and squeeze her breasts with their clamped nipples, powerfully thrusting into her from behind.

Even worse, Bella couldn't help but wonder if she would ever find herself in a similar position, probably with Alex in her place and the Wolf in Jordan's. Something inside of her quivered and she couldn't tell if it was fear or that dark, unwanted excitement that she'd discovered inside of herself.

The hard ass-fucking that Jordan was giving Trish was actually making Bella's job slightly easier, because he was rocking Trish in a steady rhythm that Bella could follow much more easily. If she looked up she could see Jordan squeezing and kneading at Trish's breasts as he fucked her. Her nipples had turned dark pink in the clamps and the chain was jerking them in every direction as her breasts were played with and bounced. Bella's own nipples throbbed in sympathy.

And yet, Trish was definitely coming closer to orgasm, the muffled noises from behind her gag becoming louder and less pained. Bella knew that Jordan wasn't going to stop fucking Trish until Bella made her come, and she did her best to seek out Trish's clit, latching on and sucking hard. Trish's head fell back as she shuddered between the two of them, her body trying to stay close to Bella and the pleasure, even as Jordan's withdrawal had her hips pulling backward.

When Trish came, it was obvious to all of them, her body arched even more dramatically than it had before and she shuddered between them, her jerky movements somehow graceful in her ecstasy. Jordan groaned, biting down on her shoulder as he thrust, hard, several times and then held still, filling her ass with his cum. Sucking as hard as she could, Bella ignored the ache in her jaw, not wanting to give Jordan any excuse to continue punishing Trish, wanting to make sure he couldn't pretend Trish hadn't come.

To Bella's shock, as Trish's body relaxed, coming down from its euphoric high, Jordan's arm wrapped around her slender waist, helping to hold her up so that all of her weight didn't end up on her wrists. Releasing the swollen pink nub from her lips, Bella panted for breath. For the first time, she could hear some of what Jordan was saying to Trish. He was crooning in her ear about what a good girl she was.

And that weird sense of envy rose inside her again.

Especially as Jordan continued to stroke Trish's legs as he undid the restraints on her ankles, rubbing them briskly for a moment, before standing and wrapping his arm around her waist again to catch her as she sagged when he released the wrist restraints. And Bella knelt there, totally forgotten as Jordan refocused completely on the little blonde.

There was something really wrong with her for feeling a bit depressed by that.

Still, as Jordan sat down and gathered Trish onto his lap, releasing the clamps, then lowering his head to each of her nipples in turn and soothing the sore buds while she whimpered, Bella couldn't help but wish that someone was that nice to her after each of her ordeals.

Alex did his best, but he was focused on other things too.

What would it be like to be so soothed and comforted, so totally the center of one man's attention like that? It wasn't something Bella had ever experienced. Although, if she was Trish, this was not the man or the situation she'd choose to experience it in. The little blonde curled into Jordan, seeking physical contact the same way Bella did with Alex, although Alex wasn't the one who did the things to her that she needed comforting for. Then again, it wasn't like Trish had anyone else. She was all alone with Jordan, all the time.

Jordan stroked her hair, combing it out with his fingers, watching the strands of it as they fell from his hand. Maybe that was one of his kinks, Bella thought. He certainly seemed obsessed with it.

She didn't know how long she knelt there, watching them. Long enough to get her breath back. Long enough to sense the soldiers behind her getting antsy. She didn't turn to look at them. All she could do was hope that Jordan wasn't about hand her over to them.

Suddenly, he straightened, although he kept his hold on Trish, reaching up to touch his hand to his ear.

"Yes... Yes, Sir." His gaze focused back on her, for the first time in what seemed like ages, and Bella shivered as he looked her up and down. Then he looked past her to the soldiers in the doorway. "The Wolf is back. Take her to him."

When the door finally opened again, Alex was practically bouncing on his feet with anxious energy. He'd tried to sit and read, and that had worked for a while, but it also let him figure out an approximation of how much time was passing. A lot of it. Not knowing what was going on, what Bella had done or what was happening to her.

Two soldiers entered and flanked the door as Nurse Roche walked in. The older woman smirked at him as he automatically tensed, flinching at her appearance. She'd been a lot less rough with him than either the Wolf or Cora had been, but he still didn't want her anywhere near him, to be perfectly truthful.

"Hello again, my little Toy," she said, winking at him.

Alex clenched his jaw against an automatic retort. He stared at her, almost daring her to come closer. This time he wasn't restrained and the soldiers were several feet away from her. On the Moon he would have never been comfortable using any kind of violence against a woman, no matter the provocation. Here... he was willing to make some exceptions. It wasn't like the women here couldn't defend themselves. Hell, he wasn't entirely sure that he'd be able to go one on one with Cora, but he knew that whatever Nurse Roche was here for, he wasn't going to give in without some kind of a fight.

The nurse laughed, reaching into her pocket and withdrawing a syringe. "Don't look so scared Toy, I'm just here to give you a shot. A little something special that the Wolf picked up, just today... it was supposed to go to the Moon but well... he figured we needed it more."

"I'm just fine without it," Alex said roughly, backing away as she pulled the plastic covering off of the syringe's needle. Whatever it was, he didn't want it in his body. No matter what she said, he wouldn't trust her.

He knew that he wasn't really going to have a choice, but maybe if he could knock it out of her hands or something he could get some extra time... figure something out. Find some way to bargain.

"Life would be so much easier for you if you didn't fight everything," Nurse Roche said, her smile turning more cruel just before pain lanced through him, traveling from his neck along the nerve pathways all through his body. Just enough electric shock to leave him gasping for air as his knees hit the ground again.

And before he could get control back over his muscles, Nurse Roche was already beside him, wiping a small area with a wet pad that smelled of alcohol and stabbing the needle into the big muscle of his left arm. Alex grunted at the slight pinch, more angry than pained by his swift defeat.

As she stood, he caught the hem of her dress. "Where's Bella?"

"Not your concern, Toy," she said, pulling her dress out of his fingers as she patted him condescendingly on the head. "For once, you've been the good one. Enjoy it while it lasts."

Dread and helpless fury engulfed him as she left without a backward glance, the soldiers following behind her.

3

The main hall was filled with celebrating soldiers chattering and drinking. For once they all ignored Bella as she was taken up to where the Wolf was. Cora and Trace were nowhere to be seen, something she was mildly grateful for. Hopefully whatever was going to happen to her wouldn't include them. While Trace had been almost kind in some ways, Cora frightened her even more after she'd seen the redheaded crime lord with Alex. She'd been far rougher with him than even the Wolf was.

To her surprise, the Wolf smiled with pleasure when he saw her. Ignoring the restraints on her wrists, he pulled her onto his lap, cupping one of her breasts while he laughed and told jokes with the men around him. It only increased Bella's inner tension to have her breasts and nipples played with, knowing that punishment was imminent. Even if he didn't know what she'd done yet, he would soon. And going by Jordan's treatment of Trish, the consequence would be a rough one. How could it be anything but? She'd gone into passageways that she shouldn't have even known were there.

One by one, the men on the dais left to join those below, leaving her and the Wolf almost completely alone.

He pinched her nipple, making her shiver as the pain and pleasure tingled through her in tandem, an endorphin rush that was both addictive and frightening.

"So, Pet," he said, his gravelly, deep voice in her ear feeling like it was sinking into the very marrow of her bones. "I hear you've been bad."

Bella trembled. "I'm sorry... I'm sorry..." She couldn't think of anything else to say. Nothing that would help, at least.

"It was rather brilliant," he said, shifting her around on his lap so that she was angled sideways, able to look at him. Those hard green eyes seemed to bore into her. "Or it could have been, if you'd known where you were going. My room has the easiest escape exits, just in case I ever need them. If you'd kept going straight, all the way to the end, you would have ended up by the main entrance. Go all the way to the right, and it lets out into the woods." He smiled, almost conspiratorially. "I wonder if you would have dared to try opening anything from in there."

Staring at him, she couldn't help but feel her tremors increasing. Knowledge was power... but it was also dangerous. "Why are you telling me this?" she whispered, frightened of the answer but needing to ask anyway. Was she going to be the first fatality among the Wolf's captives for knowing too much? Or the first to be kept here forever?

His eyes softened slightly as his hand stroked her back, almost comfortingly. That was even scarier.

"Because, sweet girl, you're not going to remember."

The arm around her tightened as he simultaneously

cupped her jaw in his other hand, something sharp pinching at her arm. Out of the corner of her eye she could see a white lab coat and what looked like a needle, the kind they used on the Moon during those rare occasions when someone needed a shot. Bella whimpered, not understanding, terrified of what they might be injecting her with.

"Bella, look at me." The use of her name made her eyes widen even as she focused on the Wolf's calm gaze. The older man stroked her cheek with his thumb, studying her. His voice was stern, insistent. "Don't forget. You don't have to stay trapped in a dome. There's plenty of space to fly free on earth. And cages are never as safe as the animals inside them think they are."

She opened her mouth to say that she didn't understand, but her tongue felt fuzzy, as if it was swelling up to twice its size. Trying to blink away the darkness that was suddenly clouding her vision, she found that she couldn't open her eyes again and she went spiraling... spiraling... spiraling...

———

Blackness gave way slowly to light. Not bright light, at first. Just enough to rouse the senses. Sounds began to trickle in, voices talking. Not softly, but not overly loud either.

Alex groaned as he tried to move his limbs. They didn't seem to want to work. The darkness obscuring his vision went away slowly as he blinked. He was disoriented. That much he realized, but he wasn't sure what he should have been expecting. Everything felt confused.

Fuzzy shapes slowly came into focus; soldiers in

khaki, activity swirling around a dark- haired man at a desk. A large blonde man stood next to him, a small young woman with matching pale blonde hair and wearing a light-blue dress tucked under his arm.

And then he remembered.

The Wolf.

Jordan.

Trish.

Bella.

He was supposed to protect Bella and she was... she was... where?

Looking around, he couldn't see her and panic welled up in his chest. Danger... there was danger...

She'd had something she'd wanted to tell him and then they'd gone back to the room and...

and...

What?

"Ah... Toy's awake."

The Wolf's deep voice brought Alex back into focus. He felt scattered, like his thoughts were skittering across the surface of his mind without really being able to sink in. It was disconcerting, to say the least.

And there was something he couldn't remember. Something important.

"How do you feel, Toy?" The Wolf spun around in his chair and leaned forward, his forearms braced against his knees, watching Alex with a curious expression on his face. The other soldiers were gone, likely sent away, although Jordan stood behind the desk with Trish. She looked a bit flushed, shifting back and forth on her feet, although she also looked curious now that the Wolf had asked the question. So whatever was going on, she didn't know about it.

"What did you do to me?" Alex asked, pushing himself to sit upright. The inside of his mouth tasted awful, now that he noticed it. "Where's Bella?"

The Wolf smiled. "You're testing a drug for us... newly acquired, in fact. Although it's not exactly a new drug, just a revised version that was scheduled to go to the Moon."

"I don't... I can't..." Alex wrinkled his forehead. He didn't remember anything after working out in the pool this morning and going back to the room with Bella. Well, he didn't remember anything clear anyway. Just that Bella had something to tell him. And flashes of her naked body entwined with his.

What the fuck had happened?

The others were watching him closely. Alex glared, clenching his fists. What the hell had they done to his memory?

The Wolf smiled, tilting his head to the side as he watched the emotions flow across Alex's face. Trish looked concerned, glancing up and Jordan and then back at Alex when Jordan didn't look at her.

"Where's Bella?"

"Pet was very, very bad. So I've sent her to the Doctor to see if he can't cure her of that."

A deep chill lanced through Alex, bringing with it a panic and a frustrated need to protect Bella, and despair because he knew that he was helpless.

"What did she do?"

Sitting back in his chair, the Wolf sighed and gave Jordan a look that Alex couldn't interpret.

———

Bella's own awakening wasn't quite as gentle as Alex's. Something—someone—was squeezing her breasts. Practically mauling them really. The heavy orbs were being squeezed and pulled and crushed with fingers. Whimpering, Bella tried to pull away, only to find that she couldn't move at all.

Her eyes snapped open and she shrieked as she looked into the dark, barren eyes of Dr. Margolis.

"Ah... the beauty finally awakens," the doctor said, pinching her nipples roughly between his fingers, hard enough to make Bella whimper again.

But she couldn't move at all. She was on her back, strapped down all over. Straps over her wrists, her ankles, her thighs, her waist, even her neck and head. There was no way she could move more than her fingers and toes. Her legs were spread, leaving her open and vulnerable.

"You've been bad, Pet," the doctor crooned, his excitement over having her at his mercy obvious, as he twisted her nipples harshly. Bella squealed and shuddered, unable to pull away from his rough handling, the swollen buds throbbing from the harsh treatment.

Her mind twisted back, away from the immediacy of her situation, in response to his accusation. How had she been bad? Their day had been completely normal, all morning, and then she'd gone to exercise and sat down with Trish... and... and...

It was a big blank. There was awareness that she was missing information, that a fair amount of time had passed between their morning outside and her current position now, but it was like trying to scale a large, smooth wall. Her memory just didn't cooperate.

"I... I don't remember," she said, her voice going high and frightened. As if she hadn't already been scared enough, just waking up face to face with the cruel doctor. She jerked against her restraints. "What did I do? What did I do that was so bad?"

The doctor just laughed at her, giving her nipples another harsh pinch that left her panting for breath as his fingers crushed the sensitive buds, holding them tightly as he cut her off from further questions. Pain filled her mind, along with the strange echoing clench of her pussy. Too much time as a captive had primed her body to certain almost survivalist responses. Her breasts and nipples were tormented, and her pussy readied itself for penetration in defense.

"You don't remember, pretty Pet?" the doctor asked, leering as he finally released her flattened nipples, making her gasp as they tingled and swelled again. "The Wolf secured a new shipment of drugs that was supposed to go to the Moon... sounds like they must be working if you can't remember what you did."

A futile sob rose up in Bella's chest, getting caught in her throat. So she was going to be punished for something she couldn't even remember doing? Whatever it was, it must have been good... or very, very bad.

Maybe she'd kicked the Wolf in his balls. The thought filled her with a savage glee, even as she silently acknowledged that it was unlikely. Such a move would be beyond stupid. And she hoped she wasn't that dumb. But what had she done that had landed her in Doctor Margolis' hands for punishment rather than the Wolf's?

"I asked for you, pretty pet," the Doctor said as he attached some strange-looking pads to the backs of his hands. His eyes never left Bella's helpless body, even as he adjusted the circular pads. "The Wolf owes me for an...

experiment I've been working on for him. And he'd been denying my request, until today."

That didn't make her feel any better. Knowing that the Wolf had been keeping her from someone, had been protecting her, only made her fear Doctor Margolis even more. She'd been frightened of him after the first time he'd been allowed to examine her, and then he'd apparently been bound by certain restrictions. There had been a solder watching that time. There was no sign of one now, although she couldn't turn her head to see behind her. Her pulse was pounding too loudly in her ears, but she couldn't hear any movement behind her either. They were alone.

And the doctor looked terrifyingly gleeful.

Fear choked her as he stood in front of her again, reaching up to cup her breasts. This time when he did so, she screamed. His hands felt like they were covered with tiny needles that pricked painfully into her skin. The shock and sting made her eyes water as she caught her breath, gasping in reaction.

What the hell?

"Electricity," Dr. Margolis said, answering her unspoken question again. His face was alight, almost joyful in the face of her pain and fear. He was avidly watching her, as if fascinated by her reaction. "One of my specialties. It can feel good..."

Suddenly the pinpricks changed to something softer, more like bubbles popping against her skin.

"Or it can hurt."

Air whistled between her teeth when she clenched her jaw against another shriek as the stabbing needles returned, feeling like they were burrowing into her soft flesh. When he pinched her nipples, it felt like tingling and heat and a stabbing lance that went straight through her body. She quivered all over, tears sliding down her cheeks as she gasped and thrashed like a fish out of water. It hurt too much for her to even try to beg or plead with him to stop, she could barely try to breathe as the ache went straight through her chest.

When he released her breasts, she sagged as much as the restraints would allow her, taking in the first deep breath that she was able to manage. Even though he'd let her go, her upper body still ached.

He trailed his fingers over her rib cage, a sizzling line that made her suck in her stomach, as if she could escape his touch.

Then, watching her face, he slid his hand further down, toward her mound.

"No, no, no, please, no," she begged, knowing it was useless but unable to stop herself as that little stinging line got closer and closer to her most sensitive tissues. She jerked against the restraints, trying to squirm away, but they were holding her far too tightly.

His fingers made a V, sliding over each side of her pussy lips and making Bella arch and shriek as the pricks of electricity snapped against the outer folds. Still watching her, his face alight with sexual excite-ment at her torment, the doctor slid his fingers between her lips, letting the electricity crackle against the soft, inner labia. Bella shrieked even louder. She didn't understand why it hurt her so badly when he didn't seem to feel it at all. His finger probed, forcing its way into her channel and she automatically clenched around him. The fact that she was wet despite the pain was humiliating.

It felt like stinging bees, in her most vulnerable area,

and Bella's tears leaked down into her hair as she begged him to stop.

Instead, he just hit a button on the table, forcing her legs to spread even further, making her even more vulnerable to him.

"Stop, please nooooooooooooooo...." Bella howled as he thrust a second finger inside of her body, fucking her with the stabbing knives of his fingers.

Then, just as suddenly, the sensation changed back to the popping bubbles. Pleasurable. Her pussy clenched again, and this time because it felt like his fingers were moving inside of her even though they weren't. It felt like her g-spot was vibrating. Bella cried out as his thumb pressed firmly against her clit. The sudden switch from pain to pleasure had her reeling with shock, as well as relief and arousal. Anything but the pain...

When Dr. Margolis did move his fingers, the sensation made Bella shudder as pleasurable flutters shot through her. The relentless pressure on her clit had tension winding around inside her, building toward orgasm as his fingers also stroked her g-spot, thrusting with fizzing pleasure.

"Nooooo..." This time she was saying it for a different reason, begging her body not to respond. She didn't trust the sadistic doctor or the pleasure that was coursing through her at his hands. But her pussy lips had plumped, her darkened nipples were erect and throbbing, and she could feel the spasms that signaled her oncoming orgasm.

Agony spiked into her, stabbing through her clit and g-spot and Bella screamed so loudly that it hurt her throat, but not nearly as much as her poor pussy was throbbing. The intense torment of his fingers against her pleasure-spots, stabbing them with electric shock, right when she'd been about to orgasm and was at her most sensitive and vulnerable, was overwhelming. Her body didn't know how to react. It spasmed, clenching, the way it would have for ecstasy, as if caught up in an orgasm made of pain.

When he finally released her, Bella was sobbing, quivering. Her body felt the same kind of tension release, the same limpness that usually followed her climaxes, but everything was different. That had hurt. More than she could have imagined.

Her pussy lips felt tight and swollen, as did her nipples, but otherwise she was physically unscathed. It almost didn't seem fair to know that there would be no sign of what she had just endured, even though it was the worst thing she'd experienced since arriving at the Wolf's compound.

The table cranked and her legs were spread farther again and lifted slightly.

"Oh god, please no…. Stop, I can't take any more…"

"That's not true, pretty pet," Dr. Margolis said, sounding both satisfied and eager as he moved down the table, ducking around her slightly elevated leg to stand directly in front of her spread pussy.

Bella whimpered as he reached out to stroke her folds again, but this time she felt nothing but the warm brush of human fingers against the tormented flesh. She stifled a cry as he thrust his fingers back inside of her, watching her tears as he fucked her with them, this time without the benefit of any electrical stimulation.

"And I'm nowhere near done with you yet…. I hear you're not a virgin here anymore."

His fingers had withdrawn from her pussy, sliding

down to press against her asshole. Bella didn't have the energy to try and fight the invasion, and both fingers pushed inside fairly quickly, stretching the tight hole. Dr. Margolis watched her face as he forcefully fucked her asshole with his fingers, He added a third one, twisting them back and forth and watching the small tremors that shook her body as her insides cramped and protested. Even though she did her best to remain quiet, she couldn't help the tiny gasps and mews that escaped as the sadist abused her tender hole. While it wasn't virgin anymore, it still wasn't used to the kind of treatment Dr. Margolis preferred.

Apparently deciding that he was no longer interested in fucking her ass with just his fingers, the doctor pulled them out and quickly undid the front of his pants, freeing his cock and thrusting into the loosened opening. Bella screamed as he impaled her, fast and hard, and without any extra lubrication. It felt like a burning rod was being shoved up her backside, and her body cramped and clenched, trying to force him back out as his cock burrowed much deeper than his fingers had, stretching her much wider. She tried to arch up and away, forgetting the restraints on her body and their lack of give, and she cried out as she realized there was nowhere for her to go.

Tears slid down the sides of her face again as he thrust, hard and fast, into her tight channel, making the delicate insides burn with the friction and strain of accommodating his large cock. The expression on his face was exuberant, and she had to wonder if this was what he'd been fantasizing about when she'd first been at his mercy and he'd realized that her ass was untouched.

Just as the cramps were lessening, her body adjusting, and the pain was beginning to dwindle, she felt the strangest sensation... fizzing, tingling inside of her ass, and she groaned as she realized he'd started the electricity up again. It didn't hurt, but she could feel her fear ramping up higher, her ass automatically clenching against the thought that he might shock her while he was raping her ass.

His dick felt like a hard, fizzing rod, sparking little bubbles all along the insides of her body. He reached up to grab her breasts and she felt the little bubbles popping against her skin on the outside as well, brushing along the tops of her inner thighs as he thrust and fucked her. The brush of his tingling groin against her abused clit made the little nub swell to attention, even as Bella fought against the building of pleasure.

It was like having a vibrator in her ass, but with a different sensation that was even more pleasurable than mere vibrations.

The jolt went through her like a shock, making her ass spasm and her body arch against the restraints as she cried out. It burned and stung, and she struggled to get away, despite knowing she couldn't.

And then she sagged as the pain receded, leaving her tingling again.

"Please," she begged, sobbing the word out as she gasped for air. Her anus felt like it had been burned, the sore muscle throbbing with the aftereffects of the shock. "Please doooo—OOOO!"

She screamed again as the shock flayed her inside and out, the pinching fingers on her nipples not even registering compared to the high-voltage shock that was tormenting the sensitive buds.

Dr. Margolis' cock seemed even larger, harder, inside of her this time when the pain diminished again. His thrusts were coming harder and faster, his eyes practically glowing as he watched her.

The third shock was the worst, because it wasn't nearly as painful but instead balanced right on the edge of pleasure and pain... and it went on and on as her body rocked and clenched. Dimly she was aware of the doctor's grunts of pleasure, the hot liquid sizzling inside of her ass, but mostly she was just wracked with the shuddering torment and half-realized pleasure that was confusing her senses.

When he reached down and pinched her clit between two of his electrified fingers, zapping the bundle of nerve endings, she came so hard that she blacked out as liquid spilled from her pussy over Dr. Margolis' groin.

———

A soldier came in and went directly to the Wolf's dais, where he was standing and conferring with some of his other officers. Cora was there as well, idly playing with a pen and occasionally looking over at Alex. He was positioned far enough away that he couldn't hear anything they were saying, but they could all see him. For the most part, he tried not to look at them. Catching Cora's glance was too disconcerting for him.

The soldier wasn't the first to come in and go directly to the Wolf, but for the first time the Wolf turned and looked at Alex after the soldier made his report. It was the first time that he'd acknowledged Alex's existence in at least an hour.

"Good," the Wolf said, glancing back at the soldier. "Take him."

Cora looked disappointed and Alex couldn't help a

little sigh of relief. He'd been nervously awaiting some kind of punishment, wracking his brain as if trying to force his memories back into his head. It hadn't worked. The hours remained stubbornly blank and he couldn't even get a hint of what had happened.

So he didn't protest when three soldiers escorted him out of the room, instead going quietly and willingly. He wanted to sit and think, plus he hoped they were taking him to wherever Bella was. Getting away from Cora was just a bonus. His protective side had been worrying about Bella even while the rest of him tried to figure out what it could have been that she'd done that he couldn't remember.

They escorted him back to their usual room, and Alex was relieved to see that Bella was lying on the bed on her back, asleep. She was on top of the covers and, although her nipples were a dark red and her pussy looked swollen and darkened as well, he couldn't see any immediate, terrible damage. Relief swept through him as he hurried into the room, ignoring the soldiers who closed the door behind him.

Sliding onto the bed, Alex reached out to touch Bella's shoulder, being gentle so as not to wake her, but needing to touch her to reassure himself that she was really there and she was really okay.

As soon as his hand touched her skin, she came awake with a scream, kicking out.

"Bella! Bella it's me!" Alex yelled, reaching out to grab her before she could fall off the bed.

Her eyes were red-rimmed and blinking rapidly, as if she was having trouble seeing. She gasped for breath, her movements slowing although she still held herself back.

"Bella?" he repeated, more cautiously quiet now,

holding onto her wrist so that she couldn't accidentally fling herself off the bed, but not trying to touch her in any other way. He rubbed his thumb soothingly over her pulse, which was beating so rapidly it felt like her vein was fluttering under his touch. "It's me, it's Alex."

"Alex," she whispered, peering at him.

And then she burst into tears and flung herself at his chest.

It was a while before Alex could get her to calm down enough to tell him what happened, and then he became the one who needed calming down. Not that she would say much more than she'd been sent to Dr. Margolis and the damned doctor apparently had an obsession with electricity. And that it had hurt more than anything else she'd ever experienced. If Alex ever got the chance, he was going to tear that man limb from limb.

Bella shook in his arms, whimpering anytime he needed to move even the slightest bit, clinging to him as if he was an oxygen tank and the dome was breached. As if she feared any movement on his part meant that he was going to let her go. But he didn't. He moved as little as possible, stroking her hair, murmuring how brave she was, promising that he'd protect her, even though it was a promise he knew he might not be able to keep. Whatever he needed to say or do to make her feel better.

Eventually she quieted, willing to just lie quiescent in his arms.

That's when he found out that she was suffering the same memory loss that he was. She didn't even remember what she'd done that she was being punished for.

"I hope it was something that hurt him... hurt *them* somehow," she said bitterly.

Alex didn't tell her that he didn't think so. He worried that it was something he had done, until Bella reminded him that if she'd been punished for his actions, the Wolf would have made sure to say so. And torment him with that knowledge. Which was a good point and a relief to Alex. He was also relieved that Bella was obviously thinking, battered but unbroken by Dr. Margolis' cruel treatment.

"Do you think you found a way out?" Alex asked, shifting to pull her a little bit more on top of him so that he could roll slightly onto his back and relieve some of the pressure on his shoulder. Bella rolled with him, one leg over his, her head nestled into the crook of his arm.

"I... I don't know." She frowned. "Dammit... I hate this. I hate having this huge, blank hole in my memory. Do you think this is what he does?" Her voice trembled a bit. "Do you think that when we're released, we'll get a shot, and we'll wake up on the Moon and not remember any of this?"

It made sense. It made so much sense. Such a move would make it impossible for the Wolf's victims to provide any information once they were returned to the Moon.

"But why hasn't anyone come up with an antidote?" he wondered, only realizing that he'd spoken out loud when Bella went completely still against him.

"Do you think..."

She didn't finish her sentence, but they both knew that she was thinking about the document that she'd seen on the Wolf's desk and, combined with this new development, what it might mean.

4

They were left alone for the entire evening, and the next morning Alex woke up to find Bella still wrapped around him. He wasn't surprised. The few times during the night that they'd rolled away from each other, he'd woken up to her whimpering and thrashing at the nightmares she was having. As long as she was next to him, touching him, that seemed to keep the bad dreams at bay. And he definitely didn't mind having her pressed up against him, although his cock was aching by the time he woke up.

The normal morning routine seemed to help center her too, although he made sure to stick close by her side. Fury and aggression was roiling inside of him, but he was becoming used to covering up those emotions in order to give Bella the gentleness and affection she needed. Especially today.

Jordan didn't let Trish anywhere near them during their exercise, which made Alex wonder if she knew anything about yesterday, since normally Jordan was more lax about letting Trish wander away from him while they were outside. Or maybe it was just because

Alex was sticking so closely to Bella, since Jordan did tend to keep his eye on Trish more whenever any male was around and usually it was Bella who talked to Trish while Alex exercised. Today, he'd stopped when Bella had so that they could stay together.

There was something much more vulnerable about Bella right now, as if she was brittle rather than her normal, more flexible self. He hadn't even realized exactly how strong and held together she'd been until now, when she seemed like she might be ready to fall apart at the slightest provocation. If he'd thought he'd felt protective of her before, that wasn't anything compared to how he felt now.

Even the soldiers seemed to sense something differ-ent. That or maybe they were just involved in something else, but either way, nobody hassled them as they sat underneath one of the many trees, Bella cradled on Alex's side, under his arm.

It felt nice to snuggle her. Good. Although he had to work to keep his thoughts from turning amorous and keep his cock under control. The damned ring made any swelling turn into something more and he didn't want her to feel threatened by him.

There was something different though... almost as if there should be something more between them. Like something was missing. He wasn't sure where that certainty was coming from, but he wondered if it had something to do with the blank space in their memories.

They didn't talk about that though. They talked about the Moon and their memories of growing up. He told her about the time he'd crawled into the ducts of the Moon's base and gotten lost. It was soothing to talk about the past, to forget for a little bit. Especially since everyone was leaving them alone for once.

While Alex still had the urge to work out his frustrations in the pool, he knew being there for Bella to cling to was more important right now. Because if she gave up completely, he didn't know what he would do. Even if his inherent protectiveness over her didn't exist, they leaned on each other to get through each day.

————

Every little movement out of the corner of her eye was still making her jumpy.

Surprisingly, she didn't hurt so much as she ached. A lingering soreness that had kept her from being able to keep up with Alex even the little bit that she normally did while in the pool. The ache skittered across her skin and felt like it had sunk deep down into her bones. And with it came a jumpiness, an automatic reaction to draw back or run and hide.

The only time she could relax was when Alex was wrapped up around her, because she could sense his vigilance and feel the tension in his body. And she trusted him to watch over her. If nothing else, she would know when something was coming.

She tried to concentrate on the blank space in her mind, still wanting to remember the hours that she was missing, but she struggled to focus on anything other than her fear and her memories of the painful zapping electricity that had run through her body. Pain and pleasure... all wrapped up in a sadistic package that had been seemingly designed to cause her body the most conflicting kind of damage.

Other thoughts came with that.

Wondering if the Wolf would have given her over to Dr. Margolis if she hadn't done something to deserve punishment. Wondering what she had done that would deserve that kind of treatment.

A strange kind of relief and gratitude toward the Wolf that he hadn't given her to the Doctor before... It put the Wolf's handling of her and Alex in a completely new light. One where, in some ways, he almost seemed kind.

Or maybe he just wasn't interested in the same things as Dr. Margolis. Because he seemed to like fucking with their heads more than anything. Otherwise, why would she have been given the drug to take away several hours of her life from her memory *before* she was given over to the doctor? Talk about a mindfuck. She didn't even know what she'd been punished for. If she'd been punished and then given the drug, she wouldn't have even remembered it.

Then again, that would have been pretty frightening. To have her body feel like this and not know why or what had been done to it.

So what was the Wolf? Compassionate or cruel? Although those didn't even seem like the right words. Were there words to describe his twisted brand of mind games, implications of concern and moments of brutality?

Curled up next to Alex underneath the tree, she was able to forget about it all for a little bit while they talked. She was able to think about her old life, which seemed so very far away, and get to know Alex a little better. They'd talked before, of course, but never really like this. Never the way a couple might as they got to know each other. The fact that he could make her giggle, in a situation like this, seemed even more significant than the way he made her feel safe.

After their time outside, they were brought back into the compound, heading for the main room where the Wolf so often held court, and Bella couldn't stop the fine tremor that went through her. She clung even closer to Alex. Out of the corner of her eye, she saw him glance down at her before he wrapped his arm around her again. On another day, it might have made her feel weaker, but today she needed it.

The Wolf was on the dais, along with Jordan, Cora and Trace. It took Bella a moment before she saw Trish, kneeling beside Jordan's chair rather than being on his lap. She had her head on his lap, his hand stroking through her hair. But her eyes were on Bella, her expression a combination of so many different emotions that Bella couldn't even begin to interpret. Did some of her missing memories involve Trish?

She had the feeling that they did, but she couldn't tell if it was just because of what she was picking up from looking at the other woman, if she had actually retained something during those lost hours, or if it she was just imagining it.

When Cora looked up at them, her slow smile made Bella's trembling increase.

The soldiers led them over to the side of the Wolf's dais and Alex immediately pushed Bella behind him, onto the cushions that were there. He sat on the edge, blocking her from the view of most of the room, including those sitting on the dais, with his larger body. Grabbing one of the pillows, Bella held it against her stomach, curling around it as if it was the stuffed bear she'd slept with every night when she was a child.

"It'll be okay," Alex murmured, his hands smoothing over the top of her head in much the same way that Jordan stroked Trish's.

To her relief, they were mostly ignored, other than the soldiers who were obviously keeping an eye on Alex and the occasional glance from Cora or Trace. No one seemed to be keeping an eye on her. Alex let her cuddle up to him again, one hand on her leg as she leaned against his back, but he didn't put his arm around her again. Doing so would prevent him from keeping his big body between her and the rest of the room, so she just leaned against his back, resting her head against his smooth skin and tucking her leg up where he could easily hold onto it.

The room was abuzz with noise from the rest of the soldiers at their tables, but because of the acoustics it was still possible to hear occasional snippets of conversation from the dais. Enough that Bella picked up that yesterday's mission had been successful, they'd gotten everything they'd wanted from the raid—including the drug that had been used on her and Alex—and that there was something else they were waiting for from it.

Bella wondered what the drug was actually for... and why one of the side effects was memory loss. Unless... no. Even if someone on the Moon was helping the Wolf, why would the Moon need memory-loss drugs? That made no sense. Maybe to help someone forget a trauma?

She rubbed her cheek against Alex's back, as if that could help ease the strange, sick feeling in the pit of her stomach. Too many things about the Wolf and the Moon didn't make sense. It felt like she was seeing lots of little puzzle pieces, but couldn't find any two that fit together.

It wasn't until Alex tensed and his fingers sank into her thigh that she realized how deep in thought she'd been. She'd completely stopped listening to the conversations around her. Startled, she jerked her head up, looking over his shoulder, and her heart sank when she saw Cora looking back at her. Not at Alex. At her, specifically.

"No," Bella whimpered, so softly that the only person who could possibly hear her was Alex. It was an instinctive reaction, one without hope.

"Did you have a particular choice in mind?" asked the Wolf, standing up and looking over at them, his eyes glinting appreciatively as Alex shifted, the muscles in his shoulders rippling. "I do believe Toy wants to play."

Was the Wolf trying to direct Cora? Because it was fairly obvious to Bella who Cora wanted. And she didn't think she was just being paranoid.

"Toy was quite a bit of fun," Cora started to say, just as Alex picked up a cushion and hurled it at them.

———

"Alex, no," Bella whispered behind him, shock threaded through her voice.

But it was too late.

Throwing a cushion was stupid. It would never hurt anyone, it couldn't even be constituted a threat, but it did what it was meant to do. Cora's eyes locked onto him, and she raised her eyebrows, looking both amused and intrigued. His skin crawled as both the Wolf and Cora focused on him, but he'd taken their attention away from Bella, which had been the goal.

"If Toy wants to play so badly, then I think we should oblige him," Cora said, with a smile that made Alex's fists clench, as if in preparation for a fight. Behind her, Trace scowled and leaned down to say something in her ear. Cora turned and patted his shoulder, saying something back to him.

With another wistful look toward Bella, Trace turned and loped off down the dais and into the crowd where two women immediately latched onto him. At the same time, Cora and the Wolf both refocused their attention on Alex.

The Wolf gestured to the soldiers nearby. "Take Pet to her room. We'll bring Alex to Cora's."

Even though they were being separated, Alex felt a spurt of relief. Unfortunately, Bella looked more upset than ever, tears filling her soft brown eyes as she grabbed his hand and squeezed it.

"I'm sorry, Alex, I'm so, so sorry," she whispered as the soldiers came closer.

"Worth it," he whispered back, planting a kiss on her forehead before the soldiers pulled her away.

When he looked back up at the Wolf and Cora, Cora had already turned away, but the Wolf was still watching him. There was no expression on the older man's face that Alex could read but there was something about the man's stance...

And then he turned away and the moment was lost.

Cora's room was huge. Decorative. Completely different from the room Bella and Alex occupied. As if he'd needed more indications on where he and Bella ranked in the scheme of things.

To his surprise, there was some obviously masculine clothing scattered around the room. Large masculine clothing. Was Cora sharing the room with someone? Was this why the Wolf hadn't been by the last few nights?

He hadn't seen all that much sexual tension between

the two of them; even now they were both definitely more focused on him than on each other.

The Wolf was standing just behind Alex, but he could feel the man's presence, and out of the corner of his eye he could see that the Wolf was watching him and not Cora, who had moved to the foot of her very large bed already. The bed was easily as big as the one in the room Alex and Bella shared; sized for an orgy rather than just sleeping.

Stripping off her clothing, Cora let each piece drop to the floor. She wasn't trying to be seductive—she knew she didn't need to be. Alex was relieved that his dick didn't even stir at the sight of her naked body, despite the fact that she was a very attractive woman. After what she'd done to him before, he didn't think he could take actually responding to just the sight of her.

Just as the relief washed through him, the Wolf stroked one finger along Alex's spine, making him shiver and then tense, rigidly waiting for whatever was going to happen next. Cora stood by the bed, her legs slightly spread with one foot in front of the other, hands on her hips, and a small smile curving her face as she watched them. Alex refused to turn to look at the Wolf. Stoically, he stared at a point just over Cora's shoulder, doing his best to shut both of them out.

The Wolf chuckled, never a reassuring sound. His finger stroked back down Alex's spine, barely touching him, so that all the hairs on Alex's body felt like they were standing straight up. As the Wolf's finger neared the crease of Alex's ass, it veered off, outlining the swell of Alex's buttocks. Automatically, Alex clenched, his hands balling into fists. The light touches made him want to flinch away, almost a ticklish reaction, but he refused to move.

"You were so eager before, Toy..." The Wolf's hot breath slid along the back of Alex's neck, except for where it was covered by the collar. "Perhaps you'd prefer that we trade you out for Pet instead?"

"No," Alex grated out. He wanted nothing more than to twist around and slam his fist in the Wolf's face. Damn the man and his mind games.

Across the room, Cora tapped her foot impatiently. "Put him on his knees, Scott. I want him to crawl to me."

That trailing finger skittered back up Alex's spine and then a heavy hand gripped the back of his neck. "Down, boy."

This is for Bella, Alex reminded himself as he knelt down without resisting. Some part of him didn't think the Wolf would bring Bella in, but that was the naive hopefulness of a child. Even if it had seemed like the Wolf was protecting Bella somewhat earlier, when Cora had been interested in her, that impression couldn't be trusted.

At least the floor was covered in a plush material, rather than being cold or hard. One small comfort for him.

"Come here, Toy," Cora practically purred, obviously enjoying seeing him down on his hands and knees. Her nipples were becoming more prominent, hardening into little buds, as she reveled in her dominance over him.

Feeling extremely vulnerable and exposed, with his cock and balls hanging down and his ass pointed straight at the Wolf, Alex gritted his teeth and crawled forward. He didn't bother to crane his neck to try and keep his eyes on Cora. There was no point. Staring at the floor, he just watched his hands as they sank into the softness of the carpet, and tried not to cringe as he thought about what the Wolf must be seeing from where he was still standing.

When he reached Cora's feet, he stared fixedly at a point between them. Looking up would feel too much like indicating he was ready for his next command. Fuck that. So he stared at her toes with their incongruous light-pink polish and watched the small muscles in her feet moving as she waited.

After a few moments, he heard the burbling laugh of her amusement at his stubbornness.

"You are a treat, Toy," she said, as her fingers fisted in his hair and yanked. Alex barely managed to keep from shouting out in pain; it felt like she was going to tear out his scalp. Instinctively he followed the pull, which brought him almost all the way to his feet before she jerked her arm to the right and he was forced to follow, half stumbling into the bed. Off balance, he reached out with one hand, hitting the bed from the side so that he tumbled onto his back, his legs hanging off the bed.

Snarling, he started to turn, lashing out defensively with his hand, and then his entire body jerked as the collar came painfully to life. Sizzling electricity shot through his throat, stunning him momentarily, so that he fell back, helpless.

Still laughing, Cora grabbed his ankle just as the electricity stopped. It took her mere moments, as Alex recovered, to flip him onto his stomach, attaching his ankles to the bedposts and forcibly spreading his legs apart, leaving his asshole exposed. Alex panted as the effects of the electric collar faded, gritting his teeth when Cora tugged gently on his balls. Her fingers were warm and teasing, rolling his balls between them, and he groaned as his cock to begin to swell.

He pushed back, almost as if he was pushing his ass at her, to keep his dick from becoming trapped in an uncomfortable position between his body and the bed, and then jerked forward as he felt a soft, wet lick across his sensitive anus. Every part of him was tensed, ready for pain, and instead she was confusing him with softness and pleasure.

The scraping of teeth against his thigh a moment later was more like what he expected, and he grunted as she bit down on the meaty part of his leg, hard enough that he knew it would leave a mark. It hurt, but at least it was less confusing than the way she was still gently fondling his balls, making his cock grow inside the tight confines of the cock-ring. Blood pulsed, throbbing in his ears as she licked the underside of his buttock and then bit down right where she had licked.

A shift on the mattress made Alex open his eyes. The Wolf was within reach, also naked now, and fisting his cock as he watched, his attention glued to Alex's face. Alex tried to turn away, not wanting to give the Wolf the pleasure of seeing his reactions, but the Wolf reached out to grab his hair, forcing Alex to look at him. Holding onto him with one hand, the Wolf shifted to bring his cock closer to Alex's face.

"Cora, could you secure Toy's arms? I wouldn't want him to give into temptation." The Wolf rolled the words off of his tongue, as if he was saying something seductive instead of talking about Alex's obvious desire to do him bodily harm.

Not that Alex had made a move to. As much as he wanted to, he wouldn't risk Bella getting more punishment because he'd done something stupid. But he got the feeling that the Wolf just liked adding that extra bit of humiliation and vulnerability... or maybe the Wolf was going to do something that he really didn't think Alex would like.

With his wrists cuffed behind his back, there really was nothing Alex could do to stop his tormentors now. The Wolf grinned, his green eyes glinting, as he rubbed the tip of his cock over Alex's forehead. Doing his best to ignore the sticky pre-cum that clung to his skin, Alex closed his eyes, not willing to look at the Wolf any further.

It didn't seem that the Wolf cared too much. The head of his cock rubbed over Alex's face almost carelessly as Cora's attention settled on Alex's asshole. He groaned as she tongued his anus again, the soft wet heat of her mouth feeling so good it was unsettling. The sensation made his balls tighten and his cock throb inside the tight confines of the ring around it. When his mouth opened to groan, the Wolf's cock pressed against it, the Wolf's hand tightening in warning in Alex's hair.

Keeping his eyes closed, Alex let the Wolf's cock slide between his lips. He ached to bite down on the hard rod, to try and snap it off with his teeth, but this was one of the times when he had to bend. Yield. Live to fight another day.

In his mind, Bella's image stood out like a beacon, helping him to accept his current position. He was doing this for her. To protect her.

Which is how he managed to keep his calm when the Wolf shifted beneath him, laying back on the bed as he pushed Alex's mouth down onto his cock. The musky, male scent filled Alex's nose as the thick dick filled his throat. He gurgled, struggling to pull back up without the use of his hands. He managed to get high enough to suck in some air through his nose, and then the Wolf was shoving him back down again, forcing the fat cock back down his throat.

At the same time, Cora was pushing something slick, thick and unyielding into Alex's anus, making him groan around the Wolf's cock. The vibrations of his vocal chords made the Wolf moan with pleasure. Alex's sphincter burned as it was violated; Cora was not being particularly gentle as she shoved the toy up his asshole, filling him quickly and uncomfortably. Squeezing his balls hard enough that they began to ache, his ass clenched around the invader, increasing his discomfort. He was impaled from both ends, his arms pinioned behind him. Trapped between his body and the soft sheets of the bed, his own cock was hard as a rock.

The dildo in his ass began to move back and forth; it had been liberally lubricated, but it was still uncomfortably large in his tight tunnel. He struggled to breathe, his muscles quickly growing tired from having to pull himself off of the Wolf's dick without the use of his arms. The movement made him rock against the bed, pleasant friction rubbing over his cock even while Cora twisted and squeezed his balls, mingling the pleasure and pain into a confusing swirl of sensation that would have made him breathless if he wasn't already struggling to breathe.

He felt himself giving in to the sensations, because his entire focus was just on trying to get enough air that he didn't pass out. The Wolf's fingers threaded through his hair, helping Alex to pull up enough to breathe, before shoving him back down. Alex's stomach muscles burned almost as much as his lungs; he didn't have the energy or the focus to try to fight back against Cora's toy in his ass or her tormenting hands on his balls, or even the pleasure of his cock as he rocked against the bed. Was this how Bella felt when she gave in? As if she was floating, uncaring about what was happening to her as long as she survived it? There was something freeing in it, something Alex hadn't experienced before because he was always fighting the entire experience, and he hated the loss of control as much as it was almost a relief.

There was no way of telling how long they kept him like that, the Wolf thrusting up into his mouth, Cora both torturing and pleasuring him from behind, all while Alex could concentrate on only one thing: getting enough air.

Suddenly it stopped and the Wolf was pulling Alex completely up and off of his cock, while Cora withdrew whatever it was she'd been thrusting into his ass. As the Wolf shifted, moving away and letting Alex's head drop onto the bed, Alex was panting, finally able to breathe freely. As his head began to unfuzz, he began to notice other areas of discomfort that had been less important than breathing—his legs were trembling, his asshole felt both empty and still burning, Cora's treatment of his balls had made his lower back ache up into his kidneys, and his shoulders were tense and cramped from having his hands tied behind his back as well as his exertions to leverage himself up off of the Wolf's cock for air.

Alex stifled a groan as Cora slid onto the bed, grasping his hair and yanking him up by it so that she could slide her body underneath his.

Now what?

Cora squirmed her way down, not bothering to look at Alex's face, like he was nothing more than an obstacle to get around. Until she reached his dick. And then he realized he wasn't an obstacle, just a fucktoy.

"Scott, lift him up a bit," Cora ordered.

Something pulled at his bound wrists, helping Cora to get exactly where she wanted. She squeezed his dick rather forcefully with her hand.

Alex gasped as tears sprung automatically into his eyes. Bitch.

Looking up at his face to see his reaction, Cora practically purred. One hand in his hair, the other around his dick, she wriggled until she had him exactly where she wanted him.

"Now."

The tight, wet heat of her pussy engulfed his cock. He didn't want it to feel good, but it did. There was no way to stop the insertion of his dick, not while Cora and the Wolf had complete control of his body. She moaned with pleasure as he came down on top of her, still holding his head upright and away from her body.

At this moment, with her beneath him, Alex felt like he was seeing everything through a red haze. He was furious at the pleasure coursing through his body, at his cock's happy snugness inside her pussy, and mostly at his two tormentors and their sick games. There was no doubt that Cora was getting off on more than just his pain or his cock; she liked that he didn't want to be anywhere near her but that his cock was sinking into her anyway.

"Oh yeah... fuck me, Scott..." Cora said breathlessly.

Before Alex could wonder what she meant, the Wolf's cock was at his ass and thrusting forward.

"Fuck!" Alex let out a hoarse cry as his ass was split open. The Wolf's cock was larger than whatever Cora had been fucking his asshole with, stretching the tight hole with a burning sensation that had his hips thrusting forward, burying his dick in Cora until he couldn't move away from the implacable filling of his own ass.

Even though he'd been in this position before with Bella, it felt completely different now. Cora was moaning and thrusting her hips upward, rubbing her pussy against Alex's groin. He was surrounded by their eager bodies, the only one in the triad that didn't want to be there.

Until now he hadn't realized how much having Bella by his side had helped him; having her there with and for him so that he wasn't alone. Being between Cora's feminine cries of pleasure, her encouragement for the Wolf to fuck them harder, and the Wolf's groaning grunts, was sickening.

With Bella he'd felt guilty over the sexual pleasure he derived, but at least he liked Bella, was attracted to her, had feelings for her that had been building... With Cora his only feeling was revulsion tinged with fear. But that didn't stop his cock from twitching inside of her, it didn't stop his ass from clenching around the Wolf's thrusts, and it didn't stop his own panting groans as he was wracked with pleasure and pain from both sides.

Frustration and anger grew as the Wolf pounded into him from behind, forcing him to thrust into Cora's wet, grasping cunt with hard strokes. She writhed and moaned beneath him, one hand still holding his hair, the other pinching and tugging on his nipples, occasionally making him jerk independently of the Wolf's thrusts. It was emotionally debilitating to be so out of control, and it was making him feel almost crazed even though he knew that there was nothing he could do about it.

Now that he wasn't struggling to breathe anymore,

he didn't have a distraction to help him submit to what was happening. Instead he wanted to fight back. The Wolf's hands were tight on his hips, keeping the Wolf's body away from Alex's bound hands even as he fucked Alex forcefully from behind. Caught between them, unable to escape, unable to fight back, Alex bared his teeth and growled at Cora as she looked up at him.

"Harder!" she demanded, her hips pushing up as if she wasn't being rammed with the weight of two rather large, muscular men. Her legs wrapped around both of them, her thighs pressing against Alex's sides as she reached for the Wolf with her feet.

Then, suddenly, she let go of Alex's head, letting it fall against her shoulder.

He didn't even think, didn't ponder the consequences; his frustration and anger boiled over and he sank his teeth into the meaty flesh between Cora's shoulder and neck.

A high-pitched scream right in his ear nearly made him let go. Her nails digging into his shoulders made him want to howl... but he didn't release until he felt her pussy convulse around him and realized that she was coming. Her orgasm had started when his teeth had sunk into her flesh. Cora wasn't just a sadist, she got off on feeling pain too.

The forceful contractions of her pussy milked him as she writhed and screamed, nearly making his eyes cross. Behind him, the Wolf began to pound even more forcefully into Alex's ass, spearing him from behind, filling him in a way that was both awful and ecstatic. His cock felt like it was about to be wrenched off in Cora's body, so hard it actually hurt because he wasn't able to come yet as the cock-ring squeezed him...

Alex howled as his body protested the abuse, his hips moving toward climax even as it was denied him. He could feel the ache in his cock and balls all through his legs and crawling along the skin of his back. Cora was beneath him, still in the throes of multiple orgasms, and the Wolf's cock was dragging over Alex's prostate with every thrust. He wanted to come, needed to come, and he thought he might seriously pass out if he wasn't allowed to.

The Wolf grabbed Alex's bound wrists with one hand, dragging Alex onto his cock, forcing him down on Cora with each hard thrust. It was painful hell and unending need; Alex couldn't support his own weight, or fight back... tears of rage and painful sexual need were practically blinding him.

And then hot jets of cum filled his ass and the tight leash of his cock-ring was finally released. His cry of ecstasy was garbled by the way his hot jizz seemed to burn the inside of his dick as it came rushing out. It felt like the pulsing of the Wolf's cock in his ass, filling him, was actually shooting cum straight through Alex's body and into Cora's. He clenched and shuddered between them, giving himself over to the much-needed release and allowing it to carry him away into welcoming darkness.

———

Pacing back and forth in their room, Bella rubbed her hands over her upper arms. She hated being separated from Alex, even if she was relieved that nothing awful was happening to her this time. Although the soldiers who had brought her back to the room had applied healing cream to her nipples, pussy and asshole—with great enthusiasm and fortunately only their fingers—her skin still felt achy and sensitive. Apparently the cream could only do so much against the lingering effects of electricity.

What was happening to Alex? Was he being punished? Pleasured? What was Cora doing to him? Not knowing was almost worse than when she'd had to watch him with the other woman. Her mind was spinning in all directions, full of questions.

Was the Wolf still with them? Would he make sure that Cora didn't break Alex?

He'd seemed at least somewhat concerned that Cora didn't break his 'toys,' although he also hadn't hesitated to hand her over to Dr. Margolis. What had she done, dammit?

Realizing that she was staring at the wall, Bella shook her head, trying to focus herself as she started pacing again. She didn't know why the sigil on the wall had caught her eye; they were all over the compound, and there were three of them on the walls of this room alone.

If only the sigil was a clock that she could watch, so at least she would know how long Alex had been gone and could try to anticipate how long they might keep him.

Throwing herself down on the bed, Bella stared at the wall again, her eyes absentmindedly tracing the sinuous curve of the sigil as her thoughts raced. All she could do was stay here and wait and hope that whatever was happening to Alex, it wasn't too horrible.

5

When Alex was brought back to the room, he was unconscious. Bella jumped up from the bed, shoving her fist in her mouth and biting down on it to keep from crying out. There were two soldiers that stopped at the door while the third, a huge brute of a guy, carried Alex in and put him down on the bed. Watching him warily, Bella kept to the other side of the mattress.

The big guy just flashed her an appreciative grin, taking in the sight of her naked curves with a long, lingering glance, and then one of the soldiers in the doorway coughed and he sighed and turned away. That was one nice thing about being considered the Wolf's property; his soldiers didn't touch her unless they had some kind of permission. Those who were tasked with applying the healing cream to her privates might use that to their advantage, but none of them had done more than touch her.

Unfortunately she couldn't say the same for Alex. Even in his slumber he was frowning, his brow wrinkled. And she could see why. His nipples were still hard and slightly darker than usual, but they weren't nearly as bad as his cock. Hanging limply on the ring around it, it was a dark, angry-red color, like it had been chafed, and his balls didn't look much better. Bella didn't want to cause him any more discomfort, so she just curled up next to him, touching as much of him as she could without actually putting any part of her body over him.

Now that he was back, all she could feel was a kind of contented relief. Strange to think that she could feel content under any part of these circumstances, but Alex's presence next to her made her feel that way.

A soft touch ran over her body, caressing. Bella knew she was asleep, that she was dreaming, but at least it was a nice dream for once. Hands cupped her breasts, squeezing gently, and wet warmth engulfed her nipple. She moaned, feeling a tongue lave over the swollen bud, the sensitive tip hardening and swelling.

The sheets caressed her legs as they spread open, fell open really, fingers sliding between the plump lips and stroking. Caressing.

"Yes," she said on a sigh, the movement of her own lips and the soft sound of her voice pulling her from the darkness. She opened her eyes to more darkness and realized she hadn't been dreaming.

There was no light in the room, so she couldn't see the man suckling at her breast, but somehow she knew it wasn't Alex. Reaching out to the right, she immediately found Alex's slumbering body, completely unconscious and unaware of what was happening on her side of the bed. Automatically she tried to close her legs.

Immediately, the fingers stroking her wet folds stopped, cupping her pussy and digging into the soft lips almost painfully.

"Open, Pet."

The Wolf's harsh, low voice made her shiver in the darkness, but she obeyed. And hated herself that her body remained wet and aroused as his fingers started stroking again and he lowered his mouth to her other nipple.

Trying not to whimper, she dug her fingers into the mattress on either side of her, refusing to touch the Wolf while he molested her body. Refusing to touch Alex. She was alone in the darkness with one man beside her and one on top of her. Considering what Alex had already been through today, trying to protect her, she didn't want to risk him earning more punishment if he woke up and lashed out.

Besides, it wasn't like the Wolf was hurting her right now. Which, mentally, was actually worse. Her legs were open because he'd told her to open them, his fingers sliding up and down her folds, her nipple in his mouth, and it all felt good. Pleasurable. Arousing. Especially when she couldn't see a blessed thing and everything seemed slightly unreal.

She gasped slightly when he slid one finger into her pussy, probing the wet channel, sliding his finger back and forth and fucking her with it as he sucked her nipple deep. It felt like there was a line of hot, fiery need between her nipple and where his finger was stroking inside of her. Then his mouth moved, traveling down her stomach and she stifled a groan, knowing where his tongue was going next.

"Why are you doing this?" she whispered into the darkness, feeling somehow safer asking such a question when she couldn't see him.

"Because I want to and I can."

The answer was simple. The feelings it engendered inside of her was not. She didn't want him to do this, to touch her, but she couldn't stop him, yet somehow his confidence and control also aroused a part of her. The same part that was attracted to very similar characteristics in Alex, that had been attracted to Ken's self-confidence. Even so, she wanted him to stop.

But her pussy was wet, and when he slid his tongue around the soft folds, around his finger inside of her, she moaned as the pleasure made her insides clench. The finger slid out and went lower, burrowing into the crinkled star of her anus, allowing him to fuck one of her holes with his finger while giving his mouth full access to her pussy. Bella held her legs apart, in the same position, her muscles tensing and trembling as she tried to fight the growing need in her core, tried not to feel the way his tongue rasped over her clit and caressed the soft interior of her cunt.

Her hips lifted, involuntarily, as need swelled inside of her, searching for more contact against her clit. The finger in her ass receded and then the tight hole stretched as he added a second, increasing the sensations that were coursing through her, increasing the pleasure. The slight pain of stretching was a fiery burn that enhanced the full sensation of having her asshole fingered, and her pussy clenched down as his tongue licked and explored, turning the pain into something arousing.

Over and over again, his tongue traced its way up to her clit, teasing the little bud, before sliding back down to the meat of her pussy, feasting on her sensitive folds but not giving her enough stimulation to climax. He teased and tasted her, until her fingers felt they might break because she was gripping the sheets so hard, and her jaw was tightly clenched to keep from begging him to let her come. The burning need for orgasm was becoming over-whelming, she was holding onto her self-control by a fingernail as she yearned to reach down and grab his head, to press his mouth against her swollen clit for more than the second's attention he gave it.

"Please..."

The plea escaped her lips as he did it again, flicking his tongue against her clit and then moving away imme-diately. She thought she might go mad from the pressure in her belly, the unsatisfied itch that was driving her to the brink of begging.

Apparently all he'd wanted was some sign from her that she was breaking, that he'd cracked her pride in favor of her sexual need. The moment the plea left her lips, he was crawling up her body until his mouth came down hard on hers, the head of his cock rubbing against her wet pussy.

Musk filled her nose and mouth, her own creamy sweetness, shameful and exciting all at the same time. His tongue delved between her lips, forcing the taste on her, as he pushed his hips forward and thrust into her ready pussy, muffling her scream of pleasure with his kiss.

She didn't realize it until a moment later, but her arms were up around his neck, clinging to him, her legs wrapping around the back of his legs as he began to thrust into her. By then it was too late. Her body demanded the contact, needing to push him faster, harder, into her creamy channel. Bella's hips lifted, meeting his thrusts.

In the back of her head she knew it was wrong, knew that she should pull her arms away, unwrap her legs from around his body and lay them out so that he was taking a passive participant; but the demands of her body couldn't be pushed aside so easily. Her pussy was weeping arousal, eagerly sucking him in with every wet, sloppy-sounding thrust. Bella was on fire, inside and out, as he fucked her with hard, powerful strokes.

The roughness of his initial entry had made her orgasm recede, but now it came screaming back as the pleasure washed over her. She dug her nails into his shoulders, crying out against his lips as the ecstasy bloomed and spread throughout her limbs. The pulsing of her pussy, the rasp of her clit against his body, was a primitive need that her logical brain couldn't overcome.

It didn't matter that he was the Wolf or that he was raping her, had sexually tortured her, her done both to Alex earlier that day; in the darkness he was just a body, a cock moving in and out of her, making her come over and over and over...

She felt his cock swell, the thick shaft pulsing as it forced jet after jet of his cum into her waiting pussy, which spasmed and sucked at his rod like it wanted the liquid offering. Bella clawed at his back, her body arching as the most intense wave of ecstasy yet rolled through her, sizzling along her nerve endings and draining her until her muscles unclenched and she fell, limp beneath him.

The Wolf's body hung over hers, his cock slowly shrinking inside of her, as shame replaced the pleasure she'd just been feeling. Now it was easy to let her legs and arms fall away, although impossible to erase the satisfied buzz in her core.

Dammit.

Her fists clenched.

As if he could read her thoughts, the Wolf chuckled with amusement. "Deep down, you're a fighter, aren't you, Pet? A lovely little Pet, but also a strong one."

Refusing to answer, Bella turned her head away in the darkness, even though he couldn't see her.

Shifting off of her, he settled onto the bed next to her and dragged her body into his, curling around her. It wasn't cuddling, more like dominating, forcing his presence on her when he knew she didn't want it. Bella did what she always did—perversely the opposite of what he'd just accused her off—she gave in. Didn't fight at all. Didn't react. It felt good not to react, when he'd used her own body's reactions against her just a few minutes ago.

"Jordan thinks it's going to be Toy, but my money's on you, Pet," he whispered in her ear. Bella shivered, not understanding what he was talking about. His hand stroked her stomach, caressing her curves in that same gentle way that had aroused her in her sleep.

Closing her eyes, Bella ignored the soft caresses, willing herself to sleep. Hoping that he would be gone when she woke up again.

To her relief, he was.

6

The day after Cora and the Wolf shared Alex, Cora was called away for some reason that remained unknown to Alex and Bella. Both of them were relieved. Bella didn't tell Alex about the Wolf's visit that night; there was nothing he could have done and she knew he'd be upset that he'd slept through it. Besides, she didn't think she could face the remembered shame of how much pleasure she'd received from it.

Something strange was happening to her. Throughout the day, she found herself staring at the sigil that decorated the compound's walls. It wasn't a particularly pretty sigil, just an S-shape with a horizontal bar through the top curve, but when she wasn't focused on a conversation or watching something, she would blink and realize that she'd been staring at it. Sometimes for a long time. And sometimes she felt like there was something significant about it. She just couldn't remember what.

Questioning Trish might have helped; she was becoming more and more sure that Trish knew something about whatever the Wolf had made her forget. And not just because Jordan was playing keep-away with the diminutive blonde. She just *knew* that Trish knew something. She felt it; not quite like a memory, but almost. Like, feelings that were related to a memory, even though she couldn't actually remember it. Which was weird, but she trusted that feeling. Trusted her gut.

In the afternoon, the Wolf ignored Alex, but pulled Bella onto his lap. Which always made her nervous, but especially after the night before. Her emotions were always strangely confused around the Wolf. While she knew that he could—and *would*—do anything he wanted to her, up to and including handing her back over to the sadistic doctor, for some reason she trusted that he wouldn't do anything that extreme without reason. Even if she couldn't remember what the reason was. Which made her want to cuddle up and act like a good little Pet when he had her on his lap, so that he didn't have any reason to punish her.

The absentminded caresses he gave her made it hard to concentrate on the conversations he was having with his soldiers, but she listened as much as possible. It would be even harder for Alex to hear what was being said, and she knew he'd want to know. Unfortunately, there wasn't much that she understood, because everything she overheard was completely out of context.

The Wolf had her settled on her side, her head tucked against his shoulder, but she constantly tried to peek at the desk without giving away what she was doing. Looking for more documents with the Moon government's seal.

When they'd first been caught, some part of her had been almost excited in a sick way, thinking that at least some of the mystery surrounding the Wolf would be solved. Instead, being his captive just seemed to raise more questions.

Why did the citizens on the Moon only know about the Wolf and not threats like Cora?

What mission had the Wolf and Cora teamed up for?

What had Moon documents been doing on the Wolf's desk and how had he gotten them? Why weren't they there now?

What had the Wolf made her and Alex forget?

Why was Trish treated differently?

What did the Wolf think she would be able to do better than Alex?

Being in the middle of the Wolf's headquarters didn't answer any of those questions. But it did distract her so that she was almost surprised when the Wolf's hand closed around her breast, squeezing it with intent rather than just idly stroking her the way he had been. Bella tipped her head back, tensing now that his focus was back on her.

"You're a good Pet, aren't you sweetheart?" he asked, using the kind of tone that he probably would with a real pet.

Bella wasn't stupid. She nodded her head, agreeing with him. "Yes, Sir."

"Maybe you deserve a reward for being such a good pet," he mused, his fingers seeking out and rolling her nipple between them, sending a wave of heat down through her belly. His words did nothing to relieve her tension though; the Wolf was extremely unpredictable, and Bella wasn't sure that they had the same idea of what a reward would consist of.

———

Watching the Wolf fondle Bella was not Alex's preferred way of spending his morning. The soreness that lingered from being double-teamed by the Wolf and Cora yesterday only added an edge to his frustration. The gap in his memory made him feel even more out of control. Possessive feelings over Bella were the last thing he needed to deal with, but somehow he felt like something had happened between them that they'd been made to forget. Something important, that was spurring his dislike of seeing her on the Wolf's lap.

All morning she'd been kind of quiet. Distant. Somehow, he didn't think it had anything to do with Doctor Margolis anymore. She wasn't so brittle, but she was just different. Alex couldn't quite put his finger on it.

Emotions that he couldn't control were surging up inside of him as he watched the Wolf stroke and caress her body, making him want to snatch her away from the other man. Yesterday he'd been able to protect her from further molestation; today he was being forced to witness it. Even worse, Bella didn't look entirely unhappy. She seemed calm, submissive. Like she was getting used to the way the Wolf was treating her.

Alex was starting to worry that she'd bent too much and had forgotten to keep fighting, even if only in her mind.

Seeing the Wolf whispering in her ear, he had to tamp down on his fury again. Yesterday he'd done what he'd had to do in order to protect her, setting aside his own need for control and letting the Wolf and Cora use him. Now he felt more out of control than ever.

He came alert as the Wolf motioned to one of his

soldiers, pushing Bella up from his lap. Something close to fear filled her eyes as she threw a glance back at Alex. Immediately he sat up on his haunches, muscles tensing. The Wolf was doing something. Alex felt like snarling when the soldier started leading Bella away, her wide eyes calling to him.

"Down, Toy." Amusement laced the Wolf's voice as he noticed that Alex was on his feet instead of sitting down the way he was supposed to be.

Alex knew he was being baited, but he didn't care. Watching Bella being taken out of the room so that he couldn't watch over her and had no idea where she was going, was shredding the last bits of his self-control.

"Where's she going?" he demanded, hating that asking the Wolf for information was the only avenue open to him. Going after her wasn't an option. The reminder of his helplessness infuriated him further. His anger was like a seething open wound, and the Wolf was prodding at it. "What are you doing to her?"

"That's not your concern."

Although it was said with complete indifference, the Wolf has swiveled around on his chair, focusing on Alex, obviously anything but indifferent. He was enjoying himself; enjoying toying with Alex, withholding information to drive him crazy. And all the while Bella was... where? Enduring what? The Wolf was playing fucking mind games again; knowing that Alex had shielded her yesterday, not allowing him to do so today.

"Where. Is. She." Alex gritted out the words between his teeth. His fists clenched at his sides, wishing that the Wolf was in arm's reach.

"Nowhere you need to worry about," the Wolf said.

He glanced over at one of the soldiers standing off to the side of Alex. "Take Toy back to their room to cool off."

"No!" Alex spun to glare at the soldier that the Wolf had given the order to, only to feel someone grabbing his arm from behind. They were closing in on him from both sides. He couldn't go back to the room, to pace and worry, only to have Bella come back to him, bruised in spirit and broken in body. Wildness rose up in him as he yanked his arm out of the grip of the soldier, turning back around to face him.

The soldier the Wolf had initially given orders to grabbed Alex from the other side, one hand on Alex's shoulder and the other on his arm. Alex snapped.

Twisting, he pulled away, using the momentum to punch the guard on his opposite side, who was already reaching for him again. The man yelled out in surprise as the satisfying thud of impact reverberated through Alex's arm. Arms wrapped around his biceps and he immediately knelt, throwing the soldier behind him off balance and flipping him over Alex's back. Adrenaline surged as another man slammed into him from behind, taking him down to the ground. Alex heard a growling noise, barely recognizing his own voice as he twisted, bringing the man down with him.

Kicking out, he felt his foot slam into somebody, heard the yelp of pain and felt the fierce rush of triumph. Finally able to fight back. Finally able to release some of the pent-up frustration that had been building inside of him for days.

A fist slammed into his side, taking away his breath, but he landed his own punch in the other man's chest, knocking him back. One of the guys down on the ground wrapped his arms around Alex's legs, taking him back down to the ground. Alex kneed him in the chin, pulling free.

That's when the Wolf finally stepped in. Three soldiers scattered back as the Wolf stepped forward, his green eyes gleaming with anticipation. Alex tensed, getting to his feet, waiting for the shock of the collar to send him back down again. Waiting for the pain. It didn't come.

"Well?" the Wolf asked, his hands hanging loosely at his sides. "This is your chance, Toy. What are you waiting for?"

Alex lunged forward, but not uncontrolled. Fuck no. If he was only going to get one chance, then he was going to make it count. He was moving with intent. Gunning right for the bastard's head.

The Wolf moved faster than Alex could believe, catching Alex's fist easily, dodging his head to the side, and at the same time twisting to throw Alex over his hip, using his own momentum against him. Shame and humiliation burned nearly as intensely as the pain of being slammed down onto his stomach, knocking the breath from him. Heat and iron pressed into him from behind, the Wolf covering Alex's body with his own, holding him against the floor.

"You're a fighter, I'll give you that," the Wolf whispered into Alex's ear, pressing the hard bulge at the front of his pants against Alex's buttocks. Alex shuddered, but his self-control was returning after the harsh dose of reality the Wolf had just given him. He was no match for a man who could move like that. "But the difference between you and me is that you've never known true desperation. You've never tasted the bitter fear that comes when you face your own death. You've never said no, not today... not me... and fought for your life. Until you do that, you'll be no match for someone like me."

The Wolf pushed Alex down as he stood up, and Alex stayed there, pressed against the floor. Not because he was acknowledging the Wolf's dominance, but because he was thinking. Assessing. No, he was no match for the Wolf, even without the collar on, but he'd been holding his own against three of the Wolf's soldiers. On the other hand, he was fairly certain they knew they weren't supposed to truly hurt him. And he'd caught them off guard. It was knowledge that he could use. That he had to use. Just because the Wolf had conquered him physically, didn't mean that Alex accepted defeat.

"Come, Toy."

As the Wolf walked away, his back to Alex, the three soldiers that had initially tried to take Alex down came to surround him. All of them were moving a bit more gingerly, one of them nursing a black eye. They glared at him, ready to pounce if he made the slightest move. Three-to-one odds without the element of surprise, especially now that the fighting adrenaline had leeched from his system, was not something Alex was stupid enough to try. Ignoring his guards, Alex padded after the Wolf.

Bella didn't realize that one of the walls was a one-way mirror. Not that she would have particularly cared if she had. She was in heaven. When the Wolf had told her that she was a good Pet, and that she'd earned a reward, she'd been both suspicious and frightened, because he hadn't told her what the reward was. Apparently, it was being pampered.

Even though she was still nervous about being separated from Alex, she was having trouble holding onto that tension through the blissful massage that she was currently receiving. Fingers dug into her back, finding every knot and soothing it away, before replacing the pressure of fingers with a stone that was almost too hot to bear. It felt lovely. The heat sank into her muscles, making her feel utterly limp on the table.

On the other side of the mirror, Alex was conflicted as hell. He hadn't been sure where the Wolf had been taking him to, but he'd hoped it would be to see what was happening to Bella. He'd honestly been expecting that it would be something horrible.

Even though he couldn't see her expression, because she was face-down on the massage table, he could tell from her soft sighs and moans that she wasn't experiencing any hardship. Indeed, the Wolf had done a complete one-eighty and was giving her an experience of pure pleasure. For some reason, it made Alex's possessive jealousy surge even higher.

The Wolf's hand clamped down on the back of Alex's neck, just above the collar. His voice was low, an intimate murmur in Alex's ear.

"Pet is being well rewarded for her behavior. I'll have to decide on an appropriate punishment for yours."

7

For several hours, Bella was in pure, relaxed bliss. She'd been massaged, oiled and pampered. The last vestiges of soreness from Dr. Margolis' sadistic treatment had been completely wiped away. The floaty high she was on felt better than any spa day she'd had on the Moon. Maybe because up there, such treatment had been normal. Taken for granted. Now she could really feel just how wonderful it truly was.

They gave her water and let her relax on a chaise that looked out into the garden area. Sure, the greenery was interspersed with soldiers, but it was still a nice view. Eventually, though, she began to feel antsy.

Standing up, she was headed toward the door to knock on it—wondering why no one had come for her yet—when it opened. As if they'd been watching and waiting for her. Somehow she wasn't totally shocked. A soldier stood in the doorway, seemingly indifferent to her naked body. Either he wasn't interested in her, or the Wolf's men were all getting used to seeing her naked anyway.

"Come with me," he said in clipped tones. Bella followed, feeling wary. They passed through several hallways, and several soldiers who leered at her, before he led her into a room that she recognized. It was the room beneath the Wolf's main one, with all the equipment for sexual pleasure and pain. Immediately she tensed, pausing on the threshold. The soldier turned back to look at her, his expression bored. "Over here."

Looking around, slightly frightened because they were alone, Bella did as he ordered. She wasn't sure what to expect now... The Wolf had said she'd be rewarded. Was that over? Was this something else? Where was the Wolf? Where was Alex? Or Jordan? Or Trish? Why was she alone with this indifferent soldier?

He didn't seem inclined to give her any answers. Grasping her wrists, he cuffed them together with wide leather restraints; the chain connecting them kept her arms about shoulder's width apart. Then he lifted her arms above her head and attached them to a hanging chain. Bella could feel her anxiety rising as she was restrained, fully aware of her vulnerability.

To her surprise, the soldier didn't even try to cop a feel. As soon as her arms were secured above her head, he just released her and walked away. Bella's jaw dropped open, but she was so surprised at his abrupt departure that the door was closing behind him before she could even think to call out after him. What was going on?

Tugging on the cuffs did nothing, of course, except make her feel even more helpless. She was completely alone, her arms secured above her head, and she had no idea if anyone even knew where she was.

"Hello?" she called out.

Another door opened in front of her, the doorway

shadowed. All she could see was the shape of a large, muscled, naked man walking toward her. But she recognized Alex, even before he stepped into the light. His expression was grim. Frightening.

"Alex?" she whispered, alarmed by the way he wasn't even looking at her. He immediately went over to one of the cabinets and pulled something out of it, before turning to approach her. Bella saw the rounded red rubber ball he was holding, leather straps hanging down from the sides of it, and her eyes widened. "Alex no... what are you doing? Please, no, Alex stop!"

But then he was in front of her and she had to stop pleading and shut her mouth, otherwise it would be all too easy for him to press the ball-gag between her lips. She stared up at him, willing him to look at her eyes, to see the pleading there... to stop and tell her what was going on.

Instead, he reached out and pinched her nipple, hard.

She gasped and the gag went in her mouth before she could blink and she made a high-pitched whining sound behind it as Alex secured it around her head.

Fear shook her; she didn't understand what was going on. Was Alex being controlled? Threatened? What was he going to do to her? And why?

Her arms were already secured and now she had no voice. She could try to kick him, but Bella knew that she was no match for him. On top of that, she couldn't quite bring herself to do it. Alex was her friend, her ally, someone that she'd come to care for, maybe even as something *more*. Trying to actually harm him seemed incomprehensible to her.

Straps went around her waist and then around her thighs and ankles, all of which had metal loops that Alex attached to chains hanging from the ceiling. Bella moaned behind the gag as the chains began to lift; The straps supported her, kept her from being uncomfortable, but she was left suspended and splayed, with her legs wide open as he attached a long bar between the straps on her ankles. She couldn't even kick out at him; the most she could do was make herself jiggle a bit in the air.

Her pulse was pounding as she watched Alex return to the drawers, looking through them for something. Even though she was afraid, she also trusted Alex not to be malicious. She knew that there had to be some reason she was doing this.

She really hoped he wasn't drugged.

Bella moaned with renewed fear as he turned, silver jewelry glinting in one hand, a thick butt plug in the other. She wriggled in the restraints; the way the straps supported her meant that her pussy and ass cheeks were splayed wide open, completely vulnerable to whatever Alex might do to her. He still wouldn't look at her, which was probably the scariest part of all.

Ducking under her suspended legs, Alex crouched below her, his face on level with her pussy. Something— his thumb—rubbed over her anus and she shivered. It didn't feel bad, but that plug had looked huge and she didn't want it inside of her.

"Is she wet?"

The Wolf's voice floated on the air from behind her, and Bella's entire body tensed. How had she not realized that he was in the room with them? Maybe because she'd been so focused on Alex. She'd assumed the Wolf was watching, but she hadn't realized that he was actually there.

"Yes." Alex's voice was a growl, filled with anger, and Bella shivered again.

She shook her head, wanting to deny that she was somehow turned on by the situation; but her body had responded to being vulnerable to Alex. To being tied up and helpless at his hands.

The Wolf made a satisfied noise behind her, and went silent again.

Something cool pressed against her anus and Bella immediately stiffened, remembering the size of the plug. Her sphincter burned as it was opened anyway, despite the tight clench of her muscles, and then she felt herself relaxing as the intruder didn't grow in size and she realized that Alex was using his finger, loosening her up. It was cool because he'd coated it in lube. The burning receded as her muscles unclamped, leaving her feeling full and strangely good as Alex's finger burrowed deeper.

It slid back and forth, letting her adjust to its size, and then he added another one. The feeling of fullness expanded, and she could feel her pussy becoming even wetter as Alex fingered her ass. It was very different from anyone else touching her there; much more erotic, even with the Wolf's voyeuristic presence. Bella was becoming more and more excited as Alex fucked her ass with his fingers, even though she was still scared because she didn't know what was going to happen—and because she'd seen how big that plug was.

She moaned a little, although the gag muffled it, when his fingers withdrew. Her body began to tense up again as the plug pressed against her tight hole. The tip wasn't as big as Alex's fingers, but the toy's circumference got a lot wider real quick.

"Bella, relax, please." Alex's voice was soft and pleading. "I don't want to hurt you."

If she hadn't been gagged, she would have yelled at him. Easy for him to say 'relax' when she was the one having a giant plug shoved up her ass. Okay, not shoved, gently worked into, but it was still huge. Alex was thrusting it back and forth, pushing it a little bit deeper every time and making her asshole burn and ache as it struggled to widen enough for the thick toy.

Her pussy was aching emptily, even as her ass protested the invasion. Bella panted behind the gag, whimpering and groaning as she was stretched wide, feeling the sharp slices whenever the plug went a little bit deeper, forced her ass a little bit wider.

"You can do this, Bella... take a deep breath... now let it out..." As she did so, Alex pushed, and Bella cried out, her teeth biting into the gag as the plug pushed fully inside her. Her anus snapped shut behind the wide bulge, clamping down on the dip between the bulb and the base. It was uncomfortable, settling inside of her, as the muscles burned from the sharp pain of fully taking the large toy.

But at least it was over now. She thought she felt Alex leave a soft kiss on her inner thigh as he stood back up, but she couldn't be sure.

The nipple clamps were on a long chain that he'd hung over the back of his neck, so that the clamps dangled down in front of his own chest. Bella mewed, trying to get Alex to look at her, but he was still avoiding eye contact as he cupped her breasts, squeezing them gently and running his thumbs over her nipples. It felt good and Bella's head fell back, her eyes closing as he fondled her.

Something strange happened. Inside of her head. Like a flash of light that was there for a second and then gone, leaving behind the strangest impression that they had done things before. Not quite like this, but that Alex had touched her this way and she'd responded, and it had been just the two of them. He pinched her nipple, tugging on it, and she moaned, caught somewhere between the present and what seemed like something out of a dream.

"You want me, don't you? Tell me you want me."

It was Alex's voice, but when Bella opened her eyes to look at him, she realized he hadn't spoken. His jaw was clenched, lips thin, his eyes on her breasts. She'd heard his voice though; in her head. She'd *remembered*. It was from the blank spot in her memory, she was sure it was.

Then Alex bent his head and sucked her nipple into his mouth, and Bella's pussy clenched, her ass protesting as it closed tightly around the plug, and she suddenly found it hard to be excited about that one tiny memory coming through the block. Alex pulled hard on her nipple, sucking it deep, and she could feel an answering pull straight down her body into her pussy. Her head fell back as she moaned, shuddering in the hanging restraints while his tongue rasped over the sensitive bud. Releasing it with a pop, he transferred his attentions to her other nipple, and her ass clenched around the huge plug, stinging slightly so that the pleasure and pain mingled in her body.

He pinched and tugged on the nipple that he'd abandoned, creating different sensations on each side of her body, equally erotic. Even though she knew the Wolf was watching, even though she hated the plug that had invaded her ass, she couldn't stop the rising need inside of her. The pain was actually starting to feel good, because at least it filled her, as Alex played with her nipples. She hung, suspended and helpless, her pussy creaming while her nipples swelled and budded. Even knowing the clamps were coming couldn't damp her growing arousal.

When he pulled away again, she tensed, her nipples already aching from his ministrations. When he closed the clamp down around one rosy bud, she shrieked, her teeth biting into the ball gag as the painful pressure crushed the poor nubbin. The second clamp elicited a second muffled shriek. The chain hung down, cool against her belly, but her nipples and pussy felt hot. The stinging in her ass was drowned out by the painful pressure on her nipples. Looking down, she could see how flat they were, how swollen between the clamps; they were already turning a darker pink and eventually she knew they'd be red and overly sensitive.

"Enjoying yourself, aren't you, Toy?" the Wolf asked silkily, a hint of smug triumph threaded through his voice. "Pet's not the only one who's aroused."

"Fuck off."

Alex ducked under her legs, headed back toward the wall, but Bella still managed to see what the Wolf was talking about. The cock ring was gone, removed, but he was fully erect. From playing with her breasts? Or from restraining her and clamping her nipples? Bella knew that Alex was an alpha male, that he liked to be in control... and she'd found that her body responded to giving up control, even to pain. She couldn't help it, and she didn't think that Alex could either. But was he worried that he was like the Wolf because he was turned on by some aspect of this?

She turned her head to watch him pick up a flogger

from the wall, its long leather strands hanging down from his hand as he turned back toward her. A shiver went down her spine. Making urgent noises, she tried to get Alex to look at her again; she wanted him to see in her face that she didn't blame him for what was happening, that she didn't blame him for getting hard. She didn't know what was going on, but she knew that it was the Wolf controlling the scene, not Alex. But he still wouldn't look at her.

The first fall of the flogger came from behind, going across her upper back. It was a soft thud, an almost gentle impact that didn't sting, but that she could still feel down into her bones. More blows fell, leaving her skin feeling more and more sensitive as it heated under the fall of leather. Then the flogging changed directions, hitting her from below, smacking against the cheeks of her bottom and the base of the plug in her ass.

It hurt... and it didn't. The impact was much less than a hand, but her skin felt like it was heating up, becoming more sensitized. She was much more aware of cool air moving across her skin after the flogger had touched it. When the ends snapped against her open pussy, she jerked, her hips lifting before falling back down. It stung, but almost in a good way, as if she'd been aching for some kind of touch and it didn't matter that when it came it was painful.

Suddenly Alex was moving away, heading back to the wall. Bella whined behind the gag when he picked up a crop. The thin, flexible length with the small leather pad on the end was vicious. Alex walked back around behind her, where she couldn't see him, and her body tensed again. In the position she was in, that wasn't easy to maintain, and her muscles quivered before falling back against the restraints all over her body.

THWAP!

Bella shrieked as the crop snapped against her ass, made more sensitive by the flogging. It felt like the blow had actually bitten into her skin, a sensation much more powerful than the sting she'd expected.

THWAP! THWAP! THWAP!

The crop delivered small, biting blows all across her buttocks. Alex was only hitting her with the leather-covered end of the crop, rather than the length of it, but that meant that each blow was delivered with the full force of his swing. Every time one landed, her ass clenched, making the plug jostle painfully inside of her bottom, her tight ring aching as it tried to close completely and ended up squeezing the rubber that was keeping it open. Tears began to trickle down her cheeks. It felt like he was covering her entire ass with small welts even though she could tell he was doing his best not to overlap the hits. It couldn't be easy as Bella began to squirm and writhe in her restraints, trying to escape the flurry of biting snaps against her sensitive skin.

Her tears flowed faster, dripping down to her breasts, as the blows began to land against skin that was already smarting painfully. Her struggles became wilder, making it even harder for Alex to aim correctly. The clamps on her nipples tugged painfully, increasing her distress, the chain jingling on her belly and increasing the weight pulling on her distended buds, as her breasts bounced while she struggled. Yet her muffled cries and writhing did nothing to stop the assault.

When it finally stopped, Bella sagged, struggling to breathe through her tears. She barely noticed as Alex walked around in front of her, ducking underneath the bar spreading her ankles so that he was standing within the triangle made by the bar and her legs again. He was still hard, and this time, everyone in the room knew it wasn't because of the cock-ring.

"Is she wet?"

"Yes."

"Touch her."

Bella moaned as Alex's fingers probed her slick pussy lips, confused by the swell of emotions and sensations. She loved that he was touching her, and hated that it was at the direction of the Wolf. The pain in her ass and nipples mixed with the pleasure that his stroking fingers brought her, making her pussy clamp down as one long finger pushed inside of her.

She was burning, inside and out; one kind of burning felt good, the other didn't, but it was becoming harder to tell which was which. Alex's finger pumped inside of her, his thumb brushing her swollen clit, and she felt a throbbing response in her clamped nipples as the chain on her belly quivered.

When her eyes fluttered open, she looked up, and for the first time Alex was looking back at her. His gaze was hot and hungry, but tinged with guilt. She tried to put her own arousal into her eyes, her own needy hunger for him.

A presence loomed behind her and hands brushed her sore ass cheeks; Bella shivered at even that light caress. She knew it was the Wolf, come to join them.

"Enough."

Alex stepped back and she felt the Wolf press against her from behind. He was naked and hard, his hand sliding down and between her legs to replace Alex's fingers as Alex picked up the crop again. Bella whimpered.

This time she had to look at Alex, to see the inner agony on his face as he raised the crop and brought it down hard on the top of her breast.

THWAP!

She screamed, unable to even flinch away with the Wolf pressing into her from behind. His fingers pressed into her pussy, stretching the tight hole, jostling the plug; and the heel of his hand rubbed over her clit. Bella writhed as the crop came down again on her other breast.

THWAP!

The beating began again, this time on her tender breasts. Her pussy creamed around the Wolf's fingers, his cock digging into her back, making her arch and thrust her breasts out as if asking Alex for more abuse. The entire time, she could see the way Alex's cock jerked with every blow; an angry red rod that stood out from his body, fully erect and practically pulsing with need.

The undersides of her breasts were the worst, so much more sensitive than the other areas of the soft mounds; and each snap of the crop against the tender spots made them jiggle twice as much as when the crop hit anywhere else. The clamps seemed to bite down even harder as her breasts bounced, her nipples were now an angry, throbbing red, matching the dark-red splotches that the crop was leaving behind on her pale skin. All the while, the Wolf's fingers worked busily in her pussy, his other hand wrapped around her waist. The hair on his thigh scratched against the tenderized skin of her ass, making her wriggle even more.

She almost didn't notice when Alex finally stopped cropping her breasts, not until he was stepping forward and reaching for the clamps. Immediately Bella tried to jerk back, but the Wolf's hold on her was too tight, his fingers plunging in and out of her pussy as Alex removed both the clamps at once. She spasmed, her body arching and writhing against the Wolf's fingers as blood flooded the crushed nubs, re-circulating. It felt like hundreds of tiny needles were jabbing into the poor nubbins.

Alex's hot, wet mouth sucked them gently between his lips, soothing the tortured buds, one after the other. Despite the pain, she could feel her need to come growing, stoked by the constant thrusting of the Wolf's fingers and the painful pleasure now emanating from her nipples. Just as she thought she might be approaching orgasm, the Wolf's hand pulled away and Alex straightened.

Moaning in disappointment, Bella shuddered as the restraints began to move, lifting her higher between the two men. She whined, high and shrill, as the plug was tugged from her anus, leaving the hole achingly empty. The gag was making her jaw ache, and frustrating her, because she could hear the sounds so loudly in her own head, but she knew the men couldn't.

Stepping forward, Alex placed his cock at the entrance of her pussy, and thrust inward. Bella moaned, her pussy shuddering with pleasure as it was finally filled, her nipples protesting as they brushed against his hairy chest. She began to writhe again, mewing muffled protests, as the Wolf's cock pressed against the still-tender opening of her anus. But, even though the muscle had been stretched, her pussy was now full of Alex's cock, and her asshole was going to be a tight fit.

More tears sparked in her eyes as the Wolf pushed in, relentlessly boring into her asshole as it stretched even further. Unlike the plug, his cock didn't have a nice, thinner part to relieve the pressure on her tight ring; it was just forced open as he pushed deeper and deeper. She moaned and panted, feeling almost heady with the burning pleasure as she felt the two cocks nestle next to each other inside of her body, separated only by a thin membrane. The sensations made her dizzy with confusion; it was becoming harder to tell who was doing what, which man was touching her how.

Hands gripped her ass cheeks. making her clench around both of them as pain flared, the sensitive skin protesting the tight grip. Bella shuddered as they began to move—she couldn't tell if she was feeling pleasure tinged with pain or pain edged with pleasure. Her anus spasmed as the Wolf's cock slid out and in, moving in the opposite direction of Alex's thrusts. The sensation of being always being filled, receding, pushing, using her, made her feel almost insane with the intense overload.

Muscled bodies moved, wiry hair rasping against the sensitive skin of her bottom, against her tormented nipples, pressing in around her on all sides. Hands cupped her breasts, squeezing them tightly. She was like a ragdoll between them, unable to move in the restraints, voiceless and gagged, and consumed by sensation.

They were moving faster, their rhythm becoming less predictable, less controlled. The friction was rapturous. Bella arched between them, writhing, screaming into the gag as ecstasy burned through her veins, her body clamping down to try and hold them inside of her, and riding high on the waves of pleasure as they continued to move. A hand left her breast and she was barely aware of the Wolf reaching out to grab Alex by the back of his neck, fingers woven into the younger man's hair and pulling his head back.

Alex bared his teeth as his head was forced back, growling, hands tightening on Bella's buttocks and sending a hot flash of pain through her climax, pushing her even higher.

"Fill Pet's pussy with your cum, Toy."

A cry of outrage and ecstasy filled Bella's ears. The Wolf had timed his command perfectly, with Alex already so close to orgasm that he hadn't been able to hold back. Bella cried out at the same time, muffled by the gag and completely drowned out by Alex as his cock swelled and spurted inside of her. A moment later, the Wolf followed and she thought she might actually faint from the erotically charged sensation of both men filling her at once with the jets of sticky, warm cum.

It seemed to last forever, and then it was over in the blink of an eye, and Bella was slumping in the restraints, her head tipped back and resting against the Wolf's shoulder. With her eyes barely open, she could see the look of concern on Alex's face. Too tired to even attempt to reassure him, she just let her eyes close all the way.

———

Carrying Bella back to their room, flanked by the Wolf's soldiers, Alex cuddled her close even though he knew he didn't deserve to. He was consumed by guilt, even though he'd tried to make the entire experience as pleasurable for her as possible at the end. That wasn't the problem.

The problem was how much he'd enjoyed himself.

He'd always known that he liked control during sex. That was nothing new. Even mixing a little bit of pain and pleasure wasn't completely new, although what he'd done to Bella today had been far beyond anything he'd done with any other partner.

The Wolf had given him a choice. Send Bella back to Doctor Margolis, and be forced to watch whatever he did to her. Or make her into his whipping boy, at his own hands, under the Wolf's direction. And he hadn't been allowed to explain to her what was going on or why. It had been an easy choice; sending Bella back to the doctor would break her, keeping her with him meant that at least he'd have some control over the situation.

Too bad he hadn't had any over himself.

Before Alex had walked into the room, the Wolf had removed his cock-ring. He hadn't said why, but once Bella had been restrained and helpless, it became quickly apparent. His body had responded, seeing her so vulnerable, knowing that she was at his mercy. Even with the Wolf sitting there, watching, it had been a rush of power he'd never experienced before. There had literally been nothing Bella could do to stop him, and it had made him hard.

No cock-ring, and yet his erection hadn't dwindled the entire time. Sinking into her pussy had been a relief. He didn't think he could have stopped from fucking her at that point even if he'd wanted to. Then the Wolf had gripped his head, holding him, and ordering him to come... and Alex hadn't been able to stop himself.

It had been the perfect punishment. Not only had Alex had to frighten and torture Bella, but he'd discovered something he'd never wanted to know about himself. For the first time, Alex had been forced to acknowledge that he had something in common with the Wolf.

8

When Bella woke up, she was cradled in Alex's arms in their bed. Everything was sore. Alex's body was hot against hers, his fingers idly stroking her hair. Shifting slightly she tilted her head back to look at him, and his movement abruptly stilled.

"You're awake, are you all right?" The words came out in a rush, and before she had time to answer, Alex had already pulled her in tight against his broad chest.

Bella squeaked in surprise, his arms practically forcing the air out of her lungs he was holding her so tightly. It took a moment, in her shock, to even understand what he was whispering, over and over again.

"I'm sorry, I'm so, so sorry."

Bella pushed at him. "For what?"

His hold loosened, possibly in surprise, as she kept pushing. She wanted to be able to look at him. The consternation on his face was obvious, a deep line ran across his brow as he frowned at her.

"For what I did to you. I'm so sorry. I fucked up. I

flipped out when they took you and I attacked some of the guards. The Wolf gave me a choice... It was either me or Dr. Margolis." His words were slightly broken, he couldn't look her in the eyes, but Bella quickly figured out what he was trying to say, and her breath caught in terror at the thought of being back in the hands of the sadistic doctor. "I couldn't explain... I'm so sorry."

"Alex, Alex, stop," she said, keeping her voice soothing as she pushed down her own panic hearing the doctor's name. Her hands rubbed across Alex's chest, touching him, comforting him. She could practically feel the shame and guilt emanating off of him. "It's okay. I don't blame you for what happened."

"You should."

"Stop that." She smacked him lightly. That made him look at her, finally, and she stared back earnestly. "I don't blame you. I was freaked out when they took me too. And I'd take you over the doctor any day. Okay?"

He blew out a long breath, obviously not entirely reassured, but he nodded his head. "Okay."

Snuggling back into him, Bella wrapped her arms and legs around him. He was still tense, but slowly he relaxed as she cuddled with him. His tension didn't dissipate completely though. She could tell the guilt was still eating at him. Bella grimaced, hating knowing that he was beating himself up.

"I didn't hate it," she whispered.

"What?" This time it was Alex's turn to push her away slightly, so that he could hear what she'd said.

Heat suffused her cheeks and she could barely look at him. She felt her own bit of shame at the admission, but it was true. "I didn't hate all of it." She glanced at him, but he didn't look like he was judging her. Mostly, he just looked surprised. Almost hopeful. "I trusted you not to really hurt me... besides, some of it was..." Her voice trailed off. She couldn't find the words.

Somehow Alex seemed to know what she was saying anyway. Folding her back into his arms, like she was a fragile object, he cradled her, his fingers stroking her hair again. When he whispered, she finally understood why he was feeling so guilty.

"I didn't hate all of it either."

———

Alex was spitting mad at being separated from Bella again. The night before, the Wolf had come with the cream to help her, and Alex had no choice but to watch as the man ran his hands all over her body and inside of her. All the places where Alex had hurt her, the Wolf healed her. The irony was not lost on any of them. Thankfully, after that, the Wolf had left again.

This morning had gone like any other, but then instead of being taken to the main hall, Bella was led away by other soldiers. Alex found himself in the main hall, without her. He wanted to punch someone again, but this time he resisted the impulse. It helped that the soldiers were abuzz with excitement and that he knew there was no reason for the Wolf to harm her right now. Something was happening to distract the Wolf as well; he barely glanced up when Alex when was led in.

Being separated from Bella made Alex feel jumpy. She was a soothing presence for him and not being able to watch over her, having to accept that, drove him up the wall. Something he was pretty sure the Wolf knew. Maybe today was a test to see if he'd learned his lesson from yesterday. Sitting on his usual cushion, Alex tried to focus on relaxing his muscles, one by one.

Thinking about Bella helped. Yesterday, cuddling, talking, it had felt like they were meant to be there, together. Like they were forging a connection, although truthfully, it almost felt like re-forging it. As if pieces were falling back into place.

The noise in the hall rose and Alex looked up to see what was going on. Two of the soldiers came over and quickly had him moved next to the Wolf, kneeling at his side on a cushion while the Wolf stood in front of his desk at the center of the dais. It forcibly reminded Alex of Cora's visit. Adrenaline started to hum in his veins again, panic beginning to rise as he wondered if there was more to his and Bella's separation today.

A pinch at the back of his neck made him jerk; the Wolf reached out and grabbed his hair, holding him in place. Out of the corner of his eye, just seconds later, Alex could see Nurse Roche moving away. She glanced over her shoulder and smirked at him. Fury rose up, heat filling his skin, but the Wolf's hand tightened on his hair and after a long moment, he settled down. Reacting the way he wanted to might land Bella in Dr. Margolis' hands again. And it would be Alex's fault. No more stupid risks like that. Escaping was one thing; useless battles were another.

The hot adrenaline lingered, making Alex feel jumpy, like something was crawling along his skin. He could barely focus as the doors opened, soldiers coming in with two people, a young man and woman. They looked about Alex's age, their clothing showing them clearly to be from the Moon as they were dressed in the latest and most expensive fashions. Although Alex didn't immediately recognize them, they immediately recognized him, pointing and whispering to each other.

Normally he'd be wondering why, but right now he was too busy fighting his body. The heat had spread throughout his system—not rage, but arousal. The cock-ring hadn't been put back on, but his cock had risen and was hard as a rock even though he wasn't turned on. Fuck. The nurse must have injected him with an aphrodisiac. Possibly the same one that had once been used on Bella, and he'd seen how she'd reacted to that. He fought the sensations, the urge to find something to rub his cock against.

Sweat was actually breaking out on his skin, and he could barely hear what the Wolf was saying, because it sounded like there was a roaring in his ears. His cock was turning an angry-looking red color, aching with the need to be touched. The excited babble of the young man and woman would have infuriated him if he wasn't so distracted by his body.

The floor opened and the Wolf's equipment room was raised into the center of the hall; all around it, soldiers were already starting to fondle each other, kiss each other. Alex realized that this was about to turn into one of the orgies that the Wolf was famous for. The couple were what the media called the Wolf's 'day captives'—the ones who would return to the Moon talking about the perversions and lusts of the Wolf. The ones who would confirm where Alex was.

Which made him wonder why the Wolf didn't have Bella out here as well. He also noticed that Jordan and Trish were absent.

But all of these thoughts were going through the back of his head, because his foremost thought was how badly he needed to fuck someone. Anyone.

"Go on, Toy, welcome Maureen and Zander to Earth." The Wolf pulled Alex to his feet by his hair, propelling him forward. It was like moving in a haze. A red, lust-filled haze. The Wolf's hand stayed on his lower back, guiding him.

He could feel his mind slipping away, his logic, his reason, becoming buried under primal, animal instincts.

"Holy shit," Maureen said, her eyes wide as one of the soldiers pushed her into Alex. She was a pretty little thing, with dark-red hair and hazel eyes that were tinted green. Shorter than Bella, but just as curvy. Still clothed, which Alex found enraging.

He kissed her, and she pressed her lips back against his eagerly. Her excitement was palpable, and it sickened him, but not enough to make him want to fight the effects of the aphrodisiac. The sounds of sex and passion were beginning to fill the room, he was dimly aware of the Wolf beside him, stripping Zander down. When Alex pulled away from kissing Maureen to yank her shirt off, he caught a glimpse of Zander—the slimly muscled blond was already naked and getting down on his knees in front of the Wolf. The same kind of anticipatory excitement that Maureen was exhibiting was also apparent on Zander's face.

They were obviously going through a very different experience than Alex and Bella had had when they'd first arrived. Zander was eagerly unbuttoning the Wolf's pants and Maureen clung to Alex's shoulders as she watched them.

"Oh my god," she whispered, her eyes round, her

chest heaving with excitement as Alex pushed her skirt down off of her hips. "I can't believe that's the Wolf... and we're here... holy shit, this is so sick!"

Alex wanted to tell her that it *was* sick, and not in the positive way that she'd meant. That she was sick too, being excited by the idea of danger, without actually realizing exactly how dangerous the Wolf was. She had no idea. Her pampered little world couldn't even begin to comprehend the kinds of things that Alex and Bella had been put through after being taken. Maureen knew exactly what was going on, and she was getting a thrill from the forbidden, the danger, the unknown.

If he could have found the words, he would have told her how deranged it all was. But he was too far gone into the physical effects of the aphrodisiac, his body clamoring for release. So he just pushed her over to the bed and spun her around, bending her over it so that at least he wouldn't have to look at her face.

Her skin was very pale, almost ivory in color, contrasting sharply with the dark-green color of the sheets on the bed. Her hips pushed up, eagerly, and Alex growled with both erotic need and anger. What the hell was wrong with her? And Zander? Did she not realize that he was a prisoner? Or did she find that part exciting too?

Shoving his cock forward, he wasn't at all gentle as he impaled her pussy in one hard stroke, making her quiver and cry out. But she was wet, ready, and her pussy squeezed him tightly as he pressed his body against her groin. He groaned. It felt absolutely fucking heavenly to finally get his cock into something. Need urged him onward. Gripping her hips, he started fucking her hard and fast, feeling no need to worry about her pleasure. The aphrodisiac was riding him too hard, besides which, he wasn't sure he would care anyway. It was hard to care if she got off, when emotionally he felt nothing but contempt and disgust for her.

The throaty moaning noises she started making as he fucked her just increased his disgust, but the aphrodisiac coursing through his veins meant that it didn't matter.

9

It was like watching a porno. One that made her writhe with jealousy as well as arousal. Jordan had strapped Bella down to a chair that wasn't really a chair, because the seat was split down the center; once her thighs were restrained, he'd pushed the sides open, forcing her legs apart. The chair had been placed directly in front of the vid screen, and she was finding it impossible to look away from the orgy, even as jealous hate for the petite redhead curdled in her stomach.

"Come on, little girl," Jordan said, pushing a naked Trish onto her hands and knees. He patted her bottom, urging her forward between Bella's legs. "Make Pet feel better."

Trish didn't hesitate or protest this time, and Bella wondered if she'd given up on fighting Jordan. The little blonde was positioned on all fours, ass in the air, as she began to kiss the sensitive insides of Bella's thighs, right near Bella's pussy.

Despite her jealousy, Bella was wet. She knew it

wasn't Alex's fault, and that he'd been injected with an aphrodisiac, but she hated watching it all the same. She could see the redhead moaning, enjoying Alex's forceful handling, enjoying the orgiastic pleasure that was happening all around the room. The blond man was the same, on his knees before the Wolf, sucking eagerly on the older man's cock while his eyes darted back and forth, taking in as much of the scene as he could. The Wolf was focused on Alex, his buttocks clenching as he thrust into the blond's mouth. Bella could see the entire room.

The Wolf's soldiers were all piled up on each other, naked writhing bodies, in groups of two, three and more. One woman crawled across the bed to the redhead, spreading her legs and forcing the redhead's face into her pussy; not that the redhead needed much encouragement to begin eagerly licking the soldier's wet slit.

Bella whimpered as Trish's tongue slid between her own pussy lips, dragging her attention away from the screen for just a moment. Jordan was kneeling behind the blonde, avidly watching. As usual, he wasn't at all interested in the other erotic scenes happening, his entire focus was on what Trish was doing. One hand was teasing Trish's pussy, the other gently pressed against the small of her back, keeping her from being able to buck against his hand, controlling her movements.

Liquid heat built in Bella's pussy as Trish licked her, exploring Bella's folds with long, slow swipes of her tongue. Too slow. If Bella's wrists hadn't been restrained to the chair, she would have them on Trish's head. As it was, her hips were trying to move, but all she could do was squirm slightly in the chair, trying to press more of her pussy against Trish's mouth.

Whimpering in frustration, she looked back up at the

screen, hoping it would provide some distraction. Alex was throwing his head back as he came, his muscles tensed, looking incredibly sexy in his ecstasy. The long line of his jaw was clenched, his pulse throbbing in his neck. His fingers were digging into the redhead's hips, and it was far too easy for Bella to remember how good he'd felt inside of her.

Memories clashed, like old film superimposed over another reel, as if she could see two different versions of Alex, fucking her at two different times. Yesterday and... when?

Pleasure swirled as Trish sucked on her clit, breaking up her concentration. On the screen, the Wolf beckoned to Alex. He pulled out of the redhead, who was still moaning into the soldier woman's pussy. Cum began to drip down her legs as soon as he pulled out, but his cock was still fully erect; covered in glossy pussy juices, it stood out from his body, still red and potent-looking.

As he moved away from the redhead, another of the Wolf's soldiers was already stepping up to take his place, shoving his cock into her ready pussy.

———

"Come here, Toy," the Wolf repeated, his green eyes gleaming like a panther's. The erotic sounds of sex were all around them, the wet slaps of skin on skin, of cocks thrusting into various orifices, and hot moans and grunts filled Alex's ears. His vision felt hazy, tinged around the edges with a lustful red, his body moving as if he was in a dream.

Some small voice in the back of his head screamed at him to run, but his body moved at the Wolf's command, eagerly hoping for more pleasure. Sating himself in Maureen's tight pussy had barely had an effect on the demanding need that was clawing at his insides. Already he wanted to sink his cock into someone again. If the Wolf hadn't called to him, he would probably still be pumping away at Maureen's grasping cunt.

"I think Zander would like an ass-fucking." The Wolf gripped the man's head tightly, fingers woven through the blond hair, as the man moaned throatily around the Wolf's cock. His hips tilted, pushing his ass into the air invitingly.

The same disgust he'd felt with Maureen washed through Alex. He knew that a lot of the citizens on the Moon were hedonistic; many of them came to Earth seeking adventure and pleasures that weren't available on the Moon's surface. The reactions of Zander and Maureen confirmed them as thrill-seekers. They were probably of the social group who thrived on reports of the Wolf, speculating, wishing they might be taken. Not like Bella or himself, who had taken steps to ensure they wouldn't be abducted when they'd come to Earth. Steps which had been thrown away in one night of fury, but he would have never acted like this if he'd been taken for the day.

Unlike him, Zander and Maureen weren't being compelled by drugs or threats, only by their own desires for excitement, illicit pleasures and the fifteen minutes of fame that would follow once they returned home and told the media about their experience with the Wolf.

It made him extremely ungentle as he knelt behind Zander and shoved into the other man's ass. Fortunately, because it would salve his conscious later, Zander was obviously no stranger to anal sex. Alex's cock slid in easily to the tight haven, as Zander groaned in pained pleasure, bumping the curve of his bottom against Alex's groin as the tight ring of his entrance tightened around the base of Alex's cock.

Dragging his hips back, Alex gripped Zander's and happened to look up, his gaze clashing with the Wolf's. The criminal overlord was watching Alex, rapt with attention, as if the man sucking his cock was no more than an afterthought. Just somewhere to put his dick, a hole to bring him pleasure, while he focused on what truly interested him. Alex.

His lips pulling back in a snarl, Alex glared up at the man, keeping his eye contact with the Wolf as they pummeled and thrust into Zander between them. Pleasure washed over Alex as the man writhed, his ass clenching around Alex's pistoning cock; Alex's body was caught somewhere between erotic ecstasy and pure fury.

In the back of his mind, Alex was relieved that at least Bella wasn't part of this right now.

———

As Jordan fucked Trish from behind, her licking and sucking on Bella's pussy had become more intense, her own pleasure feeding Bella's. The vibrations of her moans hummed against Bella's pussy lips and clit, her tongue questing through Bella's folds, occasionally pulling Bella's clit into her mouth and sucking hard. Jordan watched, his gaze electric with pleasure, as Trish moved her face up and down along Bella's slit.

On the screen before her, Bella could see the Wolf and Alex fucking the man between them, although it looked more like they were locked in combat than in pleasure.

The man was an afterthought, a prop. It was almost frightening, how much Alex looked exactly like the Wolf in that moment.

Not that the man cared. The expression of ecstasy on his face, as he was bounced between them, was eager and excited. He was getting off on being used by the two men, his hard cock bouncing as they thrust into him from either end, slapping up against his belly and leaking dripping spurts of pre-cum. Gasping, Bella tried to arch her hips as Trish sucked particularly hard, making her spasm as the pleasure jolted through her clit.

"Oh fuck... please..." Bella writhed as Trish sucked harder, her mouth pulling on Bella's clit. She could see Alex's look of enraged rapture as he approached his own orgasm, the Wolf watching him avidly. Her pussy was alive with pleasure, swelling, warming, as hot tingles swept through the swollen lips. The restraints chaining her to the chair didn't allow for any movement away from Trish's tormenting mouth as her orgasm crested and burst, the suction of her clit becoming painfully pleasurable in its intensity.

She cried out, trying to arch her hips, trying to slow the stabbing ecstasy as it pierced her core, spreading throughout her body in hot waves. The steady pulls on her clit made her arms and legs jerk against their bonds, needing to push Trish away. But the younger woman was already crying out into Bella's pussy, pushing her farther, as Jordan's thrusts became harder, faster, shoving her mouth against Bella's splayed parts.

The two women were coming together, Bella's juices soaking Trish's lips, Trish's vibrating moans extending the spasming shudders of Bella's climax. Jordan groaned, his fingers digging into Trish's hips as he slammed into her, rubbing his groin over the curves of her backside as he filled her with cum.

On the screen above Jordan's head, Alex was sagging over the blond man, pulling his cock from the day captive's asshole. Like before, Alex's cock was still fully erect, looking even redder from heavy use. A woman stepped up with a cloth, rubbing it over the swollen shaft and making him jerk a shudder while she cleaned him, obviously sensitive to the slightest touch after two orgasms and yet no real relief. The Wolf was extricating himself from the blond's throat, leaving the man on all fours as a woman and another man stepped up to him, eager to try out the new meat.

The redheaded woman was still on the bed, although the two men sandwiching her body had been replaced. A third was stepping up to shove his dick in her mouth. Even though she looked tired, she was moving between them all, obviously still enjoying herself. The man in her ass was slapping her cheeks, turning them a bright pink and making her body bounce up and down with each slap.

Trish's mouth dropped away from Bella's pussy, and she moaned in relief. Her overstimulated folds felt like they were swollen to twice their size. Gripping Trish's white-blonde locks, Jordan turned her around on her knees.

"Clean me off, little girl," he murmured, his expression softening as Trish began to lap at his groin, cleaning him of their combined juices. Bella could see white trails of cum dripping down Trish's thighs, sliding down to the floor. She shivered, trying not to draw attention to herself, although she didn't think she needed to worry too much. As usual, Jordan was wrapped up in Trish; he barely noticed Bella unless she did something to draw his attention.

Still, she couldn't help but reflect over the change in Trish's responses. She hadn't hesitated once. Not when Jordan had shoved her face into Bella's pussy, or now when he had her cleaning his dick of their sex. Had he brainwashed her?

Looking back up at the screen, Bella jerked against her restraints as she saw Alex now trussed up to the large wooden frame. His arms were above his head, his legs chained to the floor about shoulder-width apart, and the Wolf was whipping him with long strands of leather. It didn't look like the Wolf was hitting very hard, but the skin on Alex's back, ass and thighs was already turning pink. A woman was on her knees in front of him, her hands braced on his thighs, her head bobbing up and down as she sucked on his cock. With a twist of jealousy in her stomach, Bella recognized one of the female soldiers that was often in the gardens at the same time as them.

Bella was so engrossed in watching the Wolf flog Alex, and the woman sucking on Alex's cock as he strained and arched his back in response to the warring sensations of pleasure and pain, that she almost forgot she wasn't alone in the room. Right up until Jordan was suddenly standing in front of her, blocking out the screen as he looked down at her with a glint in his eye. He was half-hard, probably from Trish's tongue-bath, and he was holding a strange rubber toy in his hand. It looked like a cactus, with two very large prongs and one smaller one, which sat snuggled close to one of the larger ones, while the longest prong had a larger space between it and the two others. The smaller one was glistening, as though it had been covered in lube, and dread immediately curdled in Bella's stomach as Jordan knelt down.

"Wha-what are you doing?" she stammered out, her pussy and ass clenching as he tilted his head to be able to see better. There was no way for her to close her legs or protect her most private parts as he began to push the two against her holds. Her pussy was so wet that the larger prong had no problem sliding in, and her ass was no match from the slick pressure of the smaller one. She made a whining noise as they pushed in, making her asshole burn as it was forced open.

"Quiet," Jordan ordered, reaching up to pinch her nipple, hard.

Bella whimpered, but she got the message. The toys pushing into her weren't entirely comfortable, but at least they didn't hurt. That pinch to her nipple hadn't been at all friendly. Besides, it had been a stupid question; it was pretty obvious what he was doing.

Behind him, Trish was watching with what looked like a combination of sick fascination, and reluctant jealousy, as if only now realizing that she didn't like seeing Jordan touch Bella.

Which made no sense to Bella; it would be like her feeling the same jealous possessiveness over the Wolf as she did over Alex. She didn't have too much time to dwell on it as her pussy and ass were filled up by the toy, its nubby surface rubbing pleasurably over her insides, stretching them with the thick girth of the prods. Jordan did something down there, which must have attached the toy to the chair, because he moved away and the toy stayed right where it was, firmly lodged inside of her.

The third prong jutted up between her thighs, like a perverted parody of a cock. Jordan turned to Trish, holding out his hand to bring her over. She walked slowly, looking at Bella nervously.

"Climb on Pet's lap, little girl, I want to see you riding that cock,"

Jordan's deep voice made Trish shiver. She didn't look Bella in the eyes, but she obeyed, straddling the brunette's lap and placing herself over the third prong. Bella couldn't help but moan as Trish began to lower herself, making the toy move and jiggle inside of Bella. Her holes clenched down on it, making her sphincter burn as it squeezed the hard prod. Trish had to work herself up and down to fully impale herself on it, despite the lubrication from Jordan's cum in her pussy, and it bounced and moved inside Bella as well, stirring her insides with the two prongs. Standing so that he could see both of their faces, Jordan loomed over them, watching, his cock slowly hardening at the show.

"Keep bouncing, little girl, and kiss Pet."

Trish's lips were soft and they tasted like sex; musky, salty, and sweet, with just a hint of bitterness. Bella knew that she was tasting Jordan's cum on Trish's tongue, and the combined juices of two pussies, but at least this wasn't painful. And Trish was a good kisser. Their tongues danced as Trish moved up and down, her smaller breasts brushing against Bella's larger ones, their nipples rubbing against each other. The small movements that the rods made inside Bella were turning her own, even though she couldn't move. Maybe especially because she couldn't move. She could feel Jordan moving around them, securing Trish's hands to the back of Bella's chair.

A hard hand hefted her own breast, massaging it and pinching the nipple. She squirmed in the chair, as her pussy gushed, feeling answering movement in Trish.

Suddenly pain flared in the tiny bud, and Bella shrieked into Trish's mouth, who immediately pulled away. A shiny clamp was now decorating Bella's nipple, a short chain hanging from it, and Jordan was already pinching Trish's nipple, pulling her closer to Bella.

"No, please don't, Sir," Trish begged, looking up at Jordan.

"Be a good little girl and hold still," he said firmly, giving her bottom a hefty whack that had her jumping on the fake cock inside of her. Bella groaned, her holes clenching as the rods quivered inside of her. "You can take it."

The clamp closed down around Trish's nipple, connecting her to Bella's by the short chain, which was only a few inches long.

"Ow, ow, ow," Trish chanted under her breath as she squirmed, her head arching back. Her nipples were longer than Bella's and the clamp made the jutting rosebud look even more obscene, especially when it was connecting her to Bella's body. Since she was already aroused, Bella felt the clamp as a heady mix of pleasure and pain, besides which, she'd gotten used to such a dichotomy during sex. Going by Trish's reaction and the eager lust on Jordan's face, she guessed that the younger woman wasn't.

Walking around to the other side, Jordan did the same thing, connecting the two women nipple to nipple. Every time either of them moved, they both felt it as pain in the nipples and pleasure in their pussies.

Which meant they both cried out when Jordan smacked Trish's ass. Tears sparked in her big blue eyes as she jerked, her back arching, making the chain between the clamps jiggle, and both of them writhe on the fake cocks. Bella bit her lip to keep quiet as Jordan smacked Trish's ass again, pleasure and pain sizzling through her.

The prods suddenly came to life, vibrating, and both Bella and Trish moaned. Trish couldn't stop herself from writhing, going up and down slightly on the humming cock, pulling at both of their nipples.

SMACK! SMACK! SMACK!

Jordan spanked Trish's ass, hard, watching as the two women writhed in response, their bodies becoming overwhelmed by all the sensations richoting through them. Every time Trish's body would lift, in response to the hard slaps, Bella's nipples were tugged upward, but because of the restraints on the chair, her body couldn't follow. The resultant downward pull on Trish's nipples made the blonde whimper and squirm as she settled back down, relieving the pressure on both their nipples, only to be met with another hard slap to her ass. The elaborate dildos hummed inside of them, Trish's body fucking the longest shaft as Bella was only able to squirm on top of hers.

When Jordan finally stopped spanking her, Trish sagged on top of Bella for a moment, but she couldn't stop squirming. Her pussy was creaming, juices dripping down onto Bella's thighs, and both of them were beginning to throb with the need to cum. Bella moaned, trying to move on her own, needing more, and after a moment, Trish began to lift and lower again, her clamped nipples rubbing against Bella's, causing painful sparks to flare against their pleasure.

Kneeling behind her, Jordan did something to make Trish stiffen and squeal. "Please Sir, it's too big... it's too much..."

"Shhhh, it'll fit. Pet's stuffed in both holes, just ask

her." The lascivious wickedness in Jordan's voice, his eyes shining over Trish's shoulder, made Bella shudder. She tilted her head back as Jordan began to thrust into Trish, feeling his movements by the way Trish reacted, tugging on both of their nipples as she tried to relieve the pressure on her holes by moving away from Jordan's dick. It only made both girls whimper as their nipples were pulled taut by the clamps, and there was nowhere else for Trish to go.

The tugging on her nipples made Bella arch her back as she found herself focusing on the vidscreen again. Alex was coming, thrusting his hips rhythmically forward into the mouth of the woman kneeling at his feet, his ass and back bright red as the Wolf continued to rain down blows with the long strands of the leather flogger.

"Pleeeeeeeeeease," Trish begged, her voice a long squeal, going higher and higher as she arched and pulled, making Bella shriek as her distended nipples were tugged on painfully. Then Trish let out a noise like a strangled sob, her body descending, and Bella knew that she was now stuffed in both holes; the long toy in her front and Jordan's cock buried in her ass. His fingers dug into the soft flesh above her hips, pulling her down, and Bella could only feel relief as the stress on her throbbing nipples was ameliorated.

The constant stimulation was making her feel high, but she wasn't receiving enough of it to climax.

Jordan began to move, fucking Trish's ass, forcing her to fuck the cock that connected her to Bella, making both girls moan as the toy massaged their insides and their distended nipples pulled as Trish was pushed up and down. Just like before, Bella couldn't do anything but sit and take what was given to her, unable to stop the sensation or help to increase them so that she could come.

Blinking, she stared up at the screen behind Jordan, Trish's breathy moans filling her ears as she watched the Wolf laying Alex back on the bed.

His cock felt like it had been rubbed raw, just like his back did, from his shoulders down to his knees. The flogger had made his skin feel itchy, sensitive, and the scrape of soft fabric against it was like sandpaper. Just like the Wolf's hand as it brushed over the length of his dick. Even that didn't turn Alex on, he was just burning inside and out, front and back, and it was like he was losing his mind in his need to keep coming even after he'd already orgasmed. The need didn't go away; it was a hot itch that tingled up his spine and made his balls tighten, even though they were already emptied. He'd come twice in Zander's ass, and the second time he'd barely leaked a few drops.

If he hadn't been pulled away, he probably would have kept fucking the other man, but the Wolf had wanted to whip him, putting on a show while Zander and Maureen watched. They were still involved in the orgy, but they were also voyeurs, excited by witnessing the hedonistic depravity of the Wolf's court. Having been around the Wolf for so long, Alex knew it for the show that it was. Yes, the Wolf was enjoying himself, but he didn't personally care what experience Maureen and Zander had, as long as they took word of it back to the Moon. The whole thing was carefully choreographed to enhance the Wolf's reputation, to give them something to talk about.

Everyone on the Moon was so obsessed with the Wolf and his sexual excess, with the dangers of visiting Earth, with the captives that were taken... they missed everything else about him. This really was a show, a distraction, some sleight of hand. This was not the worst side of the Wolf, but it was the most visible because he made it so.

And right now, Alex was a part of it.

He couldn't even fight back as the Wolf pressed him down onto the bed. His body was throbbing with the need to come again. The woman giving him a blow job while the Wolf whipped him had made him climax, but he hadn't had any juice left to give her. And he still felt like he was about to crawl of his skin with the need that was eating him from the inside out.

The Wolf hooked his arms under Alex's legs, bending him nearly in half as he dragged Alex's ass to the edge of the bed. His cock was slick with lube, having hardened again while he'd been whipping Alex. Pressing it against Alex's ass, the Wolf grunted as he thrust forward.

Alex's body bowed under the assault, his sphincter burning as it was forced open and the Wolf's cock pushed deep in one thrust. The same way that Alex had shoved into Zander. He groaned, writhing, his hands digging into the bed rather than hitting out at the Wolf, because he needed it. The line between pain and pleasure had already blurred, and his cock pulsed as the head of the Wolf's dick rubbed over Alex's prostate.

As the Wolf began fucking him, hard and deep, Alex thought his balls might explode from the glorious pressure; he could feel them squeezing down on their own, as if they were trying to produce more sperm for him to come. Groaning, he felt himself melting into the sensations, a kind of delicious freedom roiling through him as he gave up the fight and just let the Wolf fuck his ass. The aphrodisiac made it not only easy, but necessary.

Staring up at the ceiling, Alex jerked when he suddenly heard the familiar sound of Bella's moans. It only took him a second to realize that she was on the large screen, Trish sandwiched between her and Jordan. A scene of lust and sexual torment, very similar to what he was experiencing.

Out of the corner of his eye, he could see Maureen and Zander pointing excitedly, exclaiming over the sighting of the Wolf's other captive. The soldiers around them had all settled down to just heavy petting, rather than actually fucking, taking a break so that they could fully enjoy watching Alex and the Wolf, and now Trish, Jordan and Bella. Some of the Moon couple's words drifted through Alex's consciousness; later they would enrage him although right now he could barely understand their meaning.

"It's her! It's her!"

"Oh my god that's the other one... holy shit that's hot..."

"... do you think that feels like?... that's so cool..."

"... wish they were down here... why aren't they?"

"Can we join them?"

The Wolf pounded harder into Alex's body, leaning forward and bending Alex's legs even more. His lips parted in what was almost a snarl, his eyes boring into Alex's, even as his cock invaded Alex's insides.

"Do you hear them?" he whispered, his voice filled

with the same disgust and contempt that Alex felt for the pair. "Do you begin to see?"

The words didn't make sense, not now, although they would later, and Alex could only shake his head as the Wolf forced his cock in deeper, harder. The ribbed muscles of the Wolf's belly rubbed over Alex's red, overly sensitive shaft, and he groaned, shifting and writhing as his ass clenched down and his own cock bounced between their bodies. It was pleasure and pain, fury and lust, soundless pleasure and screaming rage.

He yelled as he came, his cock jerking emptily, tiny dribbles of fluid gathering at the tip. Heat flooded his insides as the Wolf howled, throwing his head back and grinding himself against Alex's ass, his cock throbbing against the tight inner walls of Alex's body as he spewed cum into the dark hole. The sounds of orgasm filled the room, not just Alex's and the Wolf's, but the familiar breathy cry of Bella's as she came.

When Alex opened his eyes, for a moment he thought he'd gone blind, before he realized that it was just dark. His cock rubbed against the sheets as he moved, and he clenched his jaw against the whimpering groan that expanded inside of his chest. Every inch of his dick felt battered and stripped bare. After the Wolf had fucked his ass, everything had descended back into an orgy, surrounded by the sight of Bella on the screen, with Trish and Jordan. To Alex's relief, she'd never been brought down to join them.

Cold fury swept over him as he remembered the childlike excitement of Maureen and Zander. As if everything they'd witnessed was a movie or a game. They'd wanted Bella's presence, had been thrilled to see her on the screen, as if she was some kind of real celebrity and not a victim of the Wolf's cruelty.

More clearly than ever, Alex was beginning to understand how the Wolf worked. Staring up into the darkness, it was like his brain had sorted through the information when he was unconscious, and now he could see the implications, the ramifications of the Wolf's actions. Bring in the day captives, show them the debauchery, the sexual thrills that even the Moon couldn't provide, the taboo and danger the children of the Moon craved, and add in a dash of celebrity, and suddenly who cares about what else the Wolf does?

He could cover the other criminals on Earth, cover most of his own misdeeds, because what the media cared about, what the citizens of the Moon cared about, was hearing all the juicy, illicit details of the Wolf's decadent sex life. It was almost a cultural obsession at this point. Details about crimes he and his men committed only added a dash of salacious danger to the main meat of the stories that came out about him, which always revolved around the captives he took. The mystery, the fact that captives who were with him for any length of time never told their stories, only added to the intrigue and interest.

The Wolf was a smokescreen. For not only himself, but for the other crime lords on Earth also. Alex and Bella were nothing more than props, just like the captives before them.

Yet, Alex couldn't help remembering the disgust he'd felt at Maureen and Zander's flagrant interest. His contempt for their soft minds, their immature outlooks. Before being taken by the Wolf, Alex had never questioned the obsession most of the people of the Moon had with the Wolf, even if he hadn't shared it. Even then, he'd at least been intrigued by it, he'd always listened to the media stories about the Wolf. Now he felt as though those memories belonged do a different man altogether. A different man, with a different life.

The man he was now, the man he was becoming, was starting to disturb him.

10

There was... *something* about that sigil. Bella stared at it. Beside her, Alex was still asleep, looking incredibly worn out. His brow was creased, even in slumber. She wanted to reach out and smooth the wrinkles away, but she was worried about waking him up when he obviously needed the rest. So instead she stared at the wall.

No, that wasn't quite true.

She stared at the sigil.

Moving as quietly as possible, she got up out of the bed, careful not to disturb Alex, and padded over to the wall, wincing as her pussy twinged between her legs. All of her private parts were sore after yesterday, especially her nipples. Jordan had not gone easy on her or Trish, although at least they hadn't fucked for as long as Alex had. She could still barely believe how long the orgy had gone on downstairs, while Jordan had bathed her and Trish together after all the sex. He'd been remarkably solicitous, although nowhere near as tender with her as he was with the little blonde.

Tracing her fingers delicately over the sigil, she wondered why it felt familiar to touch it. Why her emotions quivered, as if it was important that she was doing this.

"What are you doing?"

Alex's voice was hoarse, rough. She turned, feeling strangely guilty, snatching her fingers away. Looking rumpled and yet still attractive, Alex was staring at her from the center of the bed, his gaze caressing her body as if he was looking her over for any signs of injury. Warmth bloomed inside her chest as she moved back toward him, wanting to feel the false safety of his arms around her.

"Trying to remember something, I think," she said, as she crawled back onto the bed. It felt so natural, so right, to just snuggle up next to him, ignoring the soreness of her nipples as they pressed against his hard chest. Maybe if she remembered something, he would too. "Something about the sigil."

He frowned and glanced over at the wall. "That thing? It's all over the place."

"I know... I just... I don't know. Maybe it's nothing." Especially if Alex couldn't remember, because whatever they'd been made to forget, both of them must have known.

He hugged her tightly, stroking his hand over her hair. "I think I figured something out."

"What?" she asked eagerly, hope sparking in her chest.

But it wasn't about the sigil or about their memory loss, it was about the Wolf. The way he manipulated the people of the Moon, using the captives as a red herring to deflect attention from his other activities and the other criminals who controlled Earth. Listening to Alex, it was like puzzle pieces coming together in Bella's head.

It all made so much sense. It even explained why no one had picked up on the connection between the Wolf and the Moon at any point, how easy it would be for him to hide his involvement with someone in the Moon government. Even if someone did find out, they would probably assume that the Moon official was trying to get the captives released. Everything everyone thought about the Wolf always revolved around the captives and the debauchery.

Only Bella, Alex, and the other captives who were held for long periods of time were in a position to see the truth, and they were definitely in the minority. Still...

"Why hasn't anyone spoken up before?" she murmured into Alex's chest hair, her fingers stroking over his skin as she thought.

"Maybe they didn't figure it out. Or maybe it's the memory drugs," Alex said tightly. His voice roughened. "We're going to get out of here, Bella. Before he can drug us. We're going to get out of here and expose him."

He made it sound so simple that for a moment Bella truly believed him. But then she remembered the Moon documents, the mystery still surrounding that. Somehow she had to figure out what was going on before they left. Not that Alex was any closer to finding an escape route.

The sigil flashed in her mind again and she shook her head to clear it.

———

They were left alone all day, which was a relief to Alex. Soldiers came by with food and the cream that they applied to each other, sighing with relief as the healing balm immediately soothed their soreness. In the afternoon, the vidscreen flicked on, showing them the news for the second time since they'd been captured.

The excitement coming off the screen, from the reporters, as well as Maureen and Zander, was palpable and it made Alex feel sick to his stomach, even as anger rose up in his chest. They confirmed that Bella and Alex had been taken by the Wolf, and glossed over exactly what had happened during the orgy, describing it in vague terms meant to tantalize. The way the Moon worked, someone would end up paying them for a more detailed description that wouldn't appear in interviews but would be disseminated throughout the population.

Sheep, all of them, with the Wolf as their shepherd. An antiquated notion for people on the Moon, but there were still herds on Earth.

Bella watched, sitting on the bed with her knees up to her chest and her chin resting atop them, her face stoic and pale. Alex found that he couldn't sit still. He was too angry, too disgusted. Especially since there was still no mention of Trish, and he knew very well that she'd come from the Moon as well. Why the disconnect? Was it only because his and Bella's families were so prominent?

Even worse was when they finally interviewed their families. They were relieved to know that Bella and Alex were alive and, basically well, and begged the Wolf to release them soon. Then the program switched over to Ken and Lisa, who said that they had "come together" in their time of distress and they didn't blame Bella or Alex for anything that they'd been forced to do in captivity. Alex sneered.

"Oh stop," Bella said quietly, in response to Alex's growling curses against his ex-girlfriend and former best friend.

He seriously hoped his parents didn't believe that bullshit for one second. "Who cares what they say anyway?

You and I know the truth."

"The truth is that there's something seriously wrong going on," Alex said shortly. It burned him to know that he'd never realized how wrong, never even looked at it, until the situation had affected him directly.

"With the Wolf?"

"No, with our fucking society!" Alex waved his hand at the screen. "With that! They're excited, can't you feel it? They're feeding off of this, not just the reporters, but everyone who's watching it. They don't care about what goes on down here on Earth, as long as it doesn't affect them."

Bella watched him pace for another long minute.

"We were the same." Her voice was barely a whisper.

"I know," Alex said, bitterly. It was the truth, and it chafed him, but he wasn't going to be a complete hypocrite and deny it. "I tell myself I wasn't as bad, because I didn't care about learning every detail, but in some ways that's almost worst. Indifference instead of interest. The Wolf is acting like some ancient Roman dictator, and we're his gladiators. We're his circus. It doesn't just distract and entertain his people, but ours too."

"When we get back to the Moon, we'll do something about it," she said, although her tone was uncertain. Because, of course, they didn't know if anyone on the

Moon was involved, or what kind of hold the Wolf might have over the Moon's government. They knew that there was some kind of connection.

They just didn't know how important that connection was.

<h1 style="text-align:center">11</h1>

"Where are we going?" asked Bella, as the soldiers escorting them took them past the door to the Wolf's main room. The throne room. Her voice was higher pitched than normal. As much as she hated the afternoons with the Wolf and his soldiers, it was something of a routine. They either went to the Wolf's main room or back to their room, and deviations from that routine were dangerous. Unpredictable. And usually heralded something very, very bad.

Glancing over at Alex, she could see that he was anxious too; but even though he was scowling, he looked like he was almost excited too. After all, they were being led to somewhere they hadn't been before. Most of the compound looked the same, but they knew the routes they usually took, they knew where the sigils on the walls were on those routes. These were new. She could almost see Alex filing all the information away into his head as he glanced around, taking in what directions other people were coming from, and the very little they could see when they happened to pass a window.

Her question went ignored, which didn't surprise her. She hadn't really been expecting a response, it had just been automatic to ask. Sometimes someone answered. Strangely, it was most often the Wolf.

"In here," one of the soldiers said, stepping aside and smirking at them as the door opened. Bella shot a look at the woman, who seemed almost sadistically happy. Whatever was beyond that doorway, it must not be good.

Stepping in ahead of Bella, Alex suddenly stopped. His shoulders were broad enough, and he was tall enough, that she couldn't see around him.

"What is it?" she whispered, peering around his arm, which had tensed. His entire body had tensed all over, in fact. As soon as she saw what he was looking at, her blood froze.

Four people looked up from where they were sitting around the room, sprawled on comfortable chaises and lounges. Two women, two men. To look at, they were just four completely normal people, relaxing and chatting in a room that was made for it. The problem was, they shouldn't have been there at all.

Prime Richard Dillon was comfortably seated on a small couch with Prime Commander Esther Marquis. Lounging on a chaise was Secondary Prime Lorena Paulson, and Minister of Earth Relations, and all too familiar to Bella, Kenneth Pratchett, Sr. Her boyfriend's—former boyfriend's—father. The leader of the Moon's government, his right-hand woman, the commanding officer of the Moon's admittedly small military force, and the man who was supposed to be the government's liaison between the Moon and Earth. All of them looking entirely too comfortable in the Wolf's compound.

Four heads turned to watch Bella and Alex's entrance,

their eyes widening as they looked over their naked bodies. Of course, the officials were all fully clothed.

"Is it that time already?" Lorena asked, pushing herself up from a lounging position to sitting. Her short brown hair swung about her face. In her late forties, Lorena looked more like a woman in her mid-twenties; she had obviously taken advantage of all of the youthening and beautifying treatments that could be had on the Moon.

A sudden hissing sound made all of them look up, including Bella and Alex. She clung to Alex's back as a barely visible mist filled the room. It smelled sickly sweet and made her skin tingle the second she took a breath, but it was filling the room so quickly that it was impossible not to breathe it in.

"What is that?" Alex asked, his voice strongly demanding. It reassured her to hear him not backing down for a moment. "What the hell are you doing here?"

"Negotiations," Ken Sr. drawled, shuddering slightly as he drew in a deep breath. None of the officials looked concerned. The Prime Commander looked more resigned than anything else; out of all of them, she was the only one who seemed uncomfortable and gave Alex and Bella an apologetic look. Richard and Lorena both looked expectant and Ken Sr. looked downright eager. He was staring straight at Bella, with eyes so much like his son's that it was disturbing; especially with the intensity of his gaze.

The tingling feeling in her body intensified and she groaned as she suddenly recognized what she was feeling. Alex was beginning to tremble under her hands and she knew what was happening.

The officials were all standing and beginning to strip

off their clothes. Alex sank to the ground in front of her, on all fours, as if he was controlling his urges by mere force of will, hanging onto his self-control by his fingernails. Bella could feel her own willpower rapidly dwindling as her nipples hardened and her pussy lips plumped. When she shifted she could feel the slick wetness that had gathered between her legs.

"Noooo." She breathed the word out on a moan, her hand coming down on Alex's shoulder and her fingers digging in. Pleadingly, she looked at Esther, a trim and fit woman who had allowed her black hair to go grey at her temples, eschewing the usual Moon obsession with youthfulness. She was the only one who looked like she might also be trying to resist the aphrodisiac that had filled the room. "Why? Why are you doing this?"

Esther bit her lip, looking ashamed, but it was Ken Sr. who answered.

"Because we have to," he said, pulling off his pants and underwear. His erection stood straight up, glistening at the tip. He didn't sound the slightest bit uncomfortable, and the way his eyes roved over her naked body made her want to throw up. Well, it made her *want* to want to throw up. She was too horny right not to feel anything but the pulsing need in her core. "The Wolf tapes all of this, you know, to ensure our silence."

"But what the hell are you doing down here in the first place?" Alex asked, his voice raspy, husky with combined fury and arousal. His head tilted up and Bella was sure that he was glaring at them. "You weren't trying to free us."

It was an accusation, hurled right at them, and the moment he said it, Bella knew it was true. They hadn't been surprised by Alex and Bella's appearance, or disturbed by the gas that filled the room. There was every indication that the officials knew exactly what was going on. That they'd done this before.

"It's the Wolf," the Prime of the Moon growled. He had pulled Esther in closer to him and was caressing her unabashedly, not even trying to fight the effects of the aphrodisiac. In fact, he looked like he was enjoying himself. At least Esther looked like she didn't want to be enjoying herself, even though she was. "He holds certain things that we need ransom. Like oxygen and food. It's a trade, we can't do anything about it."

Bella gasped. "The Moon is self-sufficient!"

That's what they'd learned in school. The Moon had hydroponics, gardens that filled the domes with air, that fed the people. Everything they could possibly need was up on the Moon, they had stopped being reliant on the earth for the necessities of life over a century ago.

Both Lorena and Ken Sr. laughed, moving toward her and Alex.

"No, it's so much cheaper to get what we need from Earth. The demands of our people are too high for us to be able to keep up with them. The size of gardens we'd need, just for the housing facilities... but that's sweet, Bella," Ken Sr. said, coming closer.

The importance of his words wouldn't be fully realized till later, when she would think about it and understand. The people of the Moon were constantly expanding, beyond what they needed or could support. They were trading with the criminal warlords on Earth to keep up the fiction. The price was their children to the Wolf, and who knew what else. And the Wolf kept them on a short leash by involving them in the captures, involving them in the depravity, so that if they ever tried to turn on them, he could show their complicity. Was it everyone? Or only these four? Then again, with these four involved, would anyone else on the Moon even need to be? Bella swayed, wanting to run, frozen in place.

Ken Sr. wrapped his hand around his cock, his eyes never leaving her face as he pumped his fist around the fat rod. "I've always thought you were sweet. Sexy."

"Leave her alone," Alex growled, starting to stand, trying to shield her from the approaching older man.

Lorena moved fast; she darted forward, pushing Alex so that he stumbled back against the door. Just as quickly, she was on her knees, sucking his cock into her mouth. He groaned, protesting, but when his hands landed on her head he wound his fingers into her hair instead of pushing her off. Bella didn't blame him; she was shaking with the need for someone to touch her pussy, to rub her swollen clit.

Even if that someone was her former boyfriend's father.

"Get away," she whispered halfheartedly as the older man finally reached her. He didn't even bother to respond, pulling her against him with one arm, his free hand latching onto her breast like a suction cup and squeezing hard enough to hurt. Bella winced and gasped, which opened her lips enough for him to thrust his tongue in.

She hated the feeling of sexual excitement that surged through her at finally being touched. The kiss was deep, and even as her brain revolted, her body thrilled at the sensation of firm fingers squeezing and kneading her breast, of the pulsing erection that was pressing against her front. The way his arm was wrapped around her lower back forced her lower body against him, making it impossible for her to pull away even if she'd had the willpower to overcome the drugs coursing through her system.

"Bring her over here, Ken," Richard said, his voice filled with lust. "I want to see the women go at it."

To Bella's relief, her ex's father pulled away from the kiss, although he groped at her ass as he pushed her toward Esther and Richard. The Prime had settled himself against the arm of the couch and he had Esther between his legs with her back against his front as he cupped and squeezed her breasts, rolling her nipples between his fingers. The woman arched her back, thrusting her breasts up into his hands, twisting slightly as her legs rubbed together, trying to put enough pressure on her clit to relieve the ache inside of her. Bella knew just how she felt.

A short, forceful shove sent her toppling on top of the other woman, putting them breast to breast, and Esther reached up to pull Bella down, melding their lips together in a kiss. Kissing her wasn't nearly as repugnant as kissing Ken Sr. had been, although Bella had another moment of shock when she realized that she was making out with the military commander of the Moon's armed forces. The leader of the Moon was now fondling both of their breasts at the same time, apparently not caring whose nipples he was pinching.

Esther's legs came up and around Bella's body so that she could rub her pussy against Bella's. They both moaned into each other's mouths as fingers pushed into their pussies simultaneously. She was no longer thinking about whose fingers they were, just about how good they felt inside of her, twisting and pushing and fucking her deep.

12

Rage only seemed to fuel Alex's lust. Even though Lorena had been the one to shove his dick down her throat, she'd lost any control she'd had the moment she'd done that. Alex was face-fucking her, slamming his cock down her throat and he didn't particularly care that she seemed to love it. He ignored her gurgles and moans, other than for the pleasure he felt as they vibrated up his cock, her vocal cords fluttering around the length of his thrusting dick. She had one hand on his thigh, uselessly trying to brace herself against him; her other hand was buried in her pussy as she pleasured herself.

As much as he wanted to go over and tear Ken's father off of Bella, he couldn't bring himself to completely pull out of Lorena's hot, sucking mouth. Even with as hard as he was using her face, his hands on the back of her head to bury his cock down her throat over and over again, her tongue kept eagerly dancing over every inch of him and she kept up a hard suction that made his knees weak.

"Fuck!" His hands tightened on her hair as he watched Ken Sr. slide his wet fingers out of the women's pussies and grab Bella's hips, lining himself up and replacing his fingers with his dick. The older man moaned as he sank into his son's ex-girlfriend's hole, throwing his head back like he was in utter ecstasy.

Growling murderously, Alex thrust hard into Lorena's mouth and groaned as he finally came, her throat quivering around his cock as he shot jet after jet of cum straight into her belly. Her throat muscles worked, and her eyes rolled up into the back of her head. That's when Alex realized she was coming too, her cries of ecstasy completely muffled by his dick, her hand furiously rubbing her clit.

Jerking her head back, he held onto his cock with one hand and slapped her across the face with it. It wasn't something he'd ever done before, but at the moment he hated her and everything she stood for, and he wanted to humiliate her the way he felt humiliated and degraded.

Lorena just whimpered and he repeated the action on her other cheek, viciously glad that he was still rock-hard and that it had to hurt at least a little. The wet smacking sound was grotesque, and she winced, but she didn't try to stop him.

"Fuck me," she gasped out, grabbing onto him when he would have tried to slide past her. Even though his brain tried to stop him, Alex found himself on his knees, between her thighs, his cock sliding into her already sopping pussy. She moaned wildly, the sound grating on his ears.

"Shut the fuck up," he growled, putting his hand over mouth so that he didn't have to listen. The heat of her pussy squeezed him so tightly that it felt like her cunt was choking his dick. With the amount of work she'd had done to the rest of her body, he felt sure that she'd had treatments to her pussy to make it tighter than it would have been otherwise. It was heaven and hell, and he wanted to pound her into the ground. He wanted her to feel him for days, and not in a good way like he would have with Bella.

Hearing Bella cry out in pleasure, he looked up to see that the foursome on the couch had shifted position slightly. Ken Sr. had dragged Bella down so that her face was level with Esther's pussy, which was filled with Richard's cock. He was still fucking her from behind as she licked Esther's clit and the base of Richard's cock as he fucked the commander.

Watching them, Alex pressed his hand down harder on Lorena's mouth as she wrapped her legs around his hips.

———

Her ex's father was fucking her... and it felt fantastic. Some part of Bella's brain was screaming with horror, while another part was eagerly moaning with pleasure, another was encompassed in watching Richard watch her between Esther's legs, and the last part, a distant part, was comparing Kento his father. Which wasn't fair, because the aphrodisiac was making her unbearably horny and sensitive, but it did seem like Ken Sr. knew just how to drag his dick out of her so that the crown rubbed over her g-spot, before shoving back into her so deep and rough that it took her breath away.

Wet fingers pressed against her anus and she wriggled, hating and loving the sensation all at once.

"Fuck yeah..." Ken Sr. said, groaning as his fingers

burrowed into her ass, his thrusts slowing so accommodate the double invasion. "I've dreamed about this ass."

Bella shuddered. That was not something she needed to know. Ever. But even with the other moans and sounds of pleasure around them, she couldn't shut out Ken Sr.'s voice.

"Bet this ass isn't virgin anymore." The smirk in his voice was humiliating. How had he even known? Her pussy clenched, as if trying to push his cock out of her, trying to push out the unwanted knowledge. "Oh yeah, prissy little Bella, I heard my son complaining to his friends about what a prude you were... wonder what he'd think if he could see you now."

Ken Sr's breath was hot on her back as he leaned over her, his thrusts coming faster and harder, his excitement over fucking her palpable. Bella sucked hard on Esther's clit, letting the other woman's loud cries of ecstasy drown out anything more that Ken Sr. might have to say to her. Her own pussy was hot and tingling, the burgeoning ache coming to a crossroads, and she knew that she wasn't going to be able to avoid coming while he fucked her.

Especially when he slid his fingers out of her ass and reached around her body, his thrusts becoming even more forceful, and he sought out her swollen clit. She cried out as he pinched the tender bud, the sharp, sudden pain setting off her orgasm, and her pussy clamped down on him as the waves of pleasure swept over her, making her buck beneath him. Groaning loudly, he tightened his grip on her young body, hips bucking as he pumped her full of his cum.

———

He could see Richard coming, but he didn't stop fucking Lorena. He was so close to orgasming again and he needed it, he could feel it like a fizzing pain in the base of his spine. The other man's cock was glossy with cream, completely coated in it, and his attention was locked onto watching Alex's cock piston in and out of Lorena's tight pussy.

It occurred to Alex that the Prime liked to watch as much as he liked to participate.

Alex nearly lost it when the man sidled behind him, and two wet fingers began to probe Alex's ass. The slight stretch and burn made his cock throb, and he was force- fully reminded of when he'd fucked Bella, just like this, and the Wolf had taken him in the ass. The Wolf, who had trapped him and Bella in a room with these assholes and drugged all of them, so that Alex and Bella couldn't even say no and mean it.

The fingers pushed deep, pressing against his prostate, and Alex groaned, his head bowing down as the movement of Richard's fingers began to dictate his thrusts into Lorena.

"That's it." The Prime's voice, so familiar from news- casts and speeches that Alex had watched over the years, washed over him. In this situation it was deeply unset- tling, and yet not nearly enough to help Alex counteract the aphrodisiac. "Fuck her hard. She likes it rough."

The fingers in Alex's ass twisted and he shouted, his body bowing as his ass cheeks clenched and cum shot up from his balls. He was completely vulnerable as he came, pumping Lorena full of her second load of cum from him, and he couldn't stop Richard from moving behind him and prying open his ass cheeks. Pain and ecstasy mingled as the other man shoved his dick into Alex's ass, making his own cock throb as his orgasm swelled even higher, like the dick in his ass was forcing the cum out of his own cock and into Lorena's pussy.

Fire and heat slid up his spine as Richard buried himself, coarse hair scraping against Alex's sensitive cheeks. His sphincter protested the suddenness of its new dimensions. Lorena writhed beneath him, even more excited now. His cock was as rock-hard as ever, despite having just filled her, and as Richard's dick dragged out of him, his own hips moved in response. It was just like being between Bella and the Wolf, except now he was glad as Richard set a pounding rhythm that made Lorena whimper as the weight of two men came down on her.

————

"That's it." Ken Sr.'s voice was filled with sick excitement. "Lick out that cream pie."

Salt, sweet, bitter musk filled Bella's mouth as she did exactly what she was told, licking Esther's pussy clean of Richard's cum. It was like her entire body was being taken over by sex, inside and out. Ken Sr. had left her pussy stuffed full of his cock and now he was grinding his body against hers, making his balls rub over her clit while she ate the older woman out.

Esther was moaning, her hands tangled in Bella's hair as she pressed the brunette into her pussy. The reluctance that she'd shown at the beginning of this had been completely wiped away by the demands of the orgy. She was moaning and rubbing her pussy up and down, practically demanding another orgasm.

Out of the corner of her eye, Bella could see Alex, trapped between the Prime and Prime Second. For a moment, she almost envied him. Ken Sr. was so focused on her that she found it incredibly disturbing, especially because he was so vocal about his sexual interest in her. She felt sick knowing that he'd fantasized about her before, while she was dating his son. He'd known that something like today was coming; had he anticipated it? Been looking forward to it?

The fact that she couldn't stop her body from responding to him only made her feel worse.

His fingers tugged at her nipples, making her clench around him as her body began to work its way toward orgasm again. Toward the pleasure that the drugs demanded. Bella moaned, sucking and licking at Esther's pussy as Ken Sr. began to slowly glide his cock back and forth inside of her, his languid thrusts pushing her face into the other woman.

Esther climaxed on Bella's tongue, again and again, while Ken Sr. fucked her, his hands rubbing all over her body. As much time as he spent squeezing and tugging on her breasts, he spent even more time squeezing her ass cheeks. Some of the time she was sure that he was holding them apart so that he could watch his cock as it pierced her pussy, other times he was more obsessed with running his thumb over the crinkled rosebud of her anus. Bella clenched every time he did so, hating the whispers that came at the same time, about how much he looked forward to fucking her sweet ass, chuckling over the fact that he knew his son hadn't.

He was sick.

And she was getting off anyway.

Suddenly Esther was moving away and Lorena was sliding into place. Bella blinked; she'd lost track of time somehow. Richard was pulling Esther from the couch to slide her in between him and Alex, stuffing her in both holes with cock. Alex was on the bottom, so that Esther was riding him, while Richard shoved into her from behind, and she screamed with pleasure at being filled so quickly.

"Suck the cum out of my pussy, pretty Pet," Lorena ordered, shoving her sloppy cunt against Bella's mouth. Cum was dripping from it, at least two loads of Alex's jizz sliding between the swollen folds. Not that Bella had much time to look at it before she was being forced to lick Lorena's slit, swallowing the warm cum as it leaked from her pussy while Lorena moaned and writhed with pleasure.

That was when Ken Sr. finally decided to pull out of Bella's pussy, and shove into her ass. She cried out as the tiny hole was stretched fast and hard, forced open by the thick girth of his penis. He burrowed in deep; no more lazy strokes, he was shoving her face into Lorena's pussy, making Bella cry out with pain and pleasure as her insides spasmed.

"Fuck, I knew you'd have a hot ass," he said, groaning as his fingers dug into her hips. "My son has no idea what he was missing."

Bella shuddered, her anus squeezing and making her burn as the friction of his cock increased when she tightened around him. It felt so good and so awful at the same time. She wanted to vomit, and instead she just kept sucking cum from Lorena's pussy, her jaw aching as she licked and sucked the older woman's folds. Lorena was moaning, loudly, playing with Bella's tits and encouraging Ken Sr. to fuck Bella's ass harder.

It was pain and pleasure, and finally Bella gave up the struggle and just let go. Almost immediately, ecstasy crashed over her and she rode the wave into oblivion.

—————

When he woke up, he didn't hurt anymore. Which was weird, because he distinctly remembered hurting in places where he hadn't known existed when he'd finally passed out.

Not gone to sleep. Passed out. In the middle of a fuck-fest that put even the Wolf's festivities to shame. He didn't know if the gas had just kept pumping into the room or what, but they'd all fucked until they'd dropped. Some of them had kept fucking after that. He'd pulled Ken Sr. off of Bella's unconscious form and bent the older man over, shoving his cock into the bastard's ass and taking far too much joy in fucking him senseless.

Alex couldn't even remember who he'd been fucking when he'd finally passed out too. He thought it might have been Esther and Richard again. His brains felt scrambled though, everything had blending together into a chaotic mess. The whole situation was FUBAR. Fucked Up Beyond All Recognition.

"We have to get out."

"What?" Bella lifted her head, blinking sleepily and looking around. She turned over, looking as though she thought the movement was going to hurt, and sighing in relief when it didn't. "They used the cream. Thank goodness."

"Yeah... but Bella, we have to escape. We have to get out of here and get back to the Moon and tell everyone." He practically yelled, enunciating the last word. There was more than just their own personal freedom at stake here; people needed to know what the fuck was going on. They needed to know that expansion of the habitat had to stop until they could support themselves, they needed to know that their resources were not what they thought they were, and they needed to know that at least four government officials were sacrificing citizens to the Wolf.

Bella's face crumpled and she shuddered, brushing her hands over her skin. He immediately felt bad, knowing that she was remembering something from yesterday. At first he reached out, but then he hesitated, not sure if she'd want to be touched at all. To his relief, Bella saw the abrupt gesture and scooted into his arms, sighing with relief as she pressed up against him.

"Are you okay?" he murmured, running his hands over her skin, as if he could brush away the memories for her.

"Yeah... I just... god, what the fuck is wrong with Ken's family? His poor mom..." Bella's voice trailed off as she shuddered.

"I know. That's why we have to escape. Bella, we have to get back home and stop this."

"We have to escape," she repeated, in a whisper.

Alex didn't even notice the odd tone to her voice.

"Yeah... just think, if we can get out of here and make it back before the Wolf memory-drugs us, we can tell everyone what's happening. We can stop it from happening to anyone else, tell them what's going on, make them understand that we have to get our resources under control so that we're not relying on the Earth anymore."

"We have to escape."

Bella sat up and Alex felt concern wash through him.

She sounded so strange, her voice taking on an almost dreamy quality as she stared across the room at the wall.

"Bella, are you okay?" he asked, brushing his hand over her shoulder.

Her forehead was creased, like her head was hurting, and she was squinting at the sigil decorating the wall. Alex turned his head to stare at it too, but whatever she was seeing, he didn't see it.

Scrambling onto all fours, Bella crawled off the bed and practically ran over to the wall. Sitting straight up on the bed, Alex watched her, confused, as she ran her fingers over the shape. Something stirred in the back of his brain, insistent but unfocused as he watched her. Like there was a hazy cloud in his mind, making it hard for him to think.

Her fingers pressed against the sigil, the right end of the bar, the left end, the bottom curve, the top curve, and then three fingers on where the S intersected. And the wall beside her opened.

Eyes wide, hand trembling, Bella turned to look at Alex, her voice a hoarse whisper. "I remember."

13

They stared at the opening in the wall, and Bella backed away, remembering what had happened the last time she'd gone into the tunnels. Memories cascaded through her, like pictures slamming down into place inside of her head. Trish. Alex. Making love. The tunnel. Jordan. Trish's punishment. The Wolf! His words...

He'd told her how to get out. *Fly free...*

"What the fuck..." Alex breathed out the words almost on a sigh. He clutched at his head and she realized he was feeling the same sensations that she had before she'd remembered. The pain, almost like a headache, but more like something was about to break through.... it had pushed at the inside of her mind like a geyser trying to burst, and once it had, she'd remembered everything.

She still didn't know how or why, but it had happened.

It was a relief, actually, to have those old memories surging up and overwhelming everything, including what she and Alex had been through the day before. She could still barely comprehend what had happened with the Moon's Prime and the others.

There was something seriously wrong with the Moon, not just the Prime, but with all its people. They'd all been ignoring the Earth, taking it for granted, taking its people for granted, and the Wolf and his ilk were the result. In some ways, she couldn't even blame him, because it was her own people who were making it possible.

How strange that even in her head, she differentiated. They were all from the same place originally, but she thought of the wealthy, pampered, sheltered people of the Moon as hers, and the more hardened people of Earth as the Wolf's. Perhaps it was just a difference in lifestyle, but in some ways, they might as well have been from entirely different worlds.

Standing, Alex distracted her as he stared at the hole in the wall, walking toward it. As he did so, the door finally closed and he stopped, looking at her. "Can you open it again?"

"Yes..." She hesitated, because she was pretty sure what his response was going to be, and that it would be a mistake. "I know how to get out."

"What?"

"I just remembered," she whispered, her eyes going back to the smooth wall where the doorway was hidden. "The Wolf told me how to reach the exits from here..."

To her relief, Alex didn't immediately demand that they use that knowledge. Which was what she had honestly expected. Sometimes he could be so single-minded. Instead, he frowned, his brow wrinkling as he processed all the new information, as well as his old memories.

"Last time, I just went exploring, and they caught me. Jordan caught me. And..." Bella's breath caught. "He punished Trish for telling me, and then the Wolf told me the fastest way to get out of the compound from here, using the tunnels. All we have to do is go straight down to the end."

"How do we know it's not another trap?" Alex muttered, but she could tell that he was asking himself, not her. Turning away, he started pacing the floor, glancing up at the ceiling in the room. They knew there were cameras up there somewhere, they just didn't know exactly where or if they were turned on.

Bella still didn't know if Jordan had come upon her by chance in the tunnels last time, or if he'd been waiting for her. She didn't really want to run the risk again though; just the thought of being returned to Dr. Margolis was enough to make her shudder.

Moving away from the door, she tried to push her fear aside.

They waited for over an hour talking through options. Discussing risks. Waiting. Wondering. Finally, Bella's stomach began growling and she realized that no one had brought them breakfast yet.

That was when the door finally opened. The regular door. The Wolf's soldiers had come for them.

———

After being fed and taken outside by the soldiers, Bella and Alex eschewed their usual workout in favor of more whispered conversation. Wondering if they'd been seen opening the passageway. Wondering what had taken so long this morning for someone to come and get them. Jordan was nowhere to be seen, and neither was Trish. Perhaps his absence had affected their schedule, rather than Bella's rediscovery of the secret passageways. There was no way of knowing.

When the soldiers led them out of the garden enclosure, Alex tensed the moment they began to bring him and Bella down a different hallway than usual. It didn't lead to the Wolf's main room, or back to their usual room, which made him immediately worry that the Wolf knew they'd found the passageway out.

He relaxed only slightly when he recognized the door they'd led them to: the Wolf's private chambers. Thanks to the healing cream, neither he nor Bella were sore from yesterday's orgy, but that didn't mean that he was looking forward to whatever twisted games the Wolf might want to play with them today.

The Wolf wasn't alone in the room either. He was laid out on the bed, his hands behind his head, looking completely relaxed as a familiar red head bobbed up and down on his cock. At the side of the bed, Trace was looming, naked and erect, looking both jealous and aroused by the sight in front of him. The moment Alex and Bella walked in, the big man's eyes flicked up to them, widened, and settled on Bella, his expression becoming more eager by the second. Alex had to stifle his own possessive growl as Trace's eyes swept up and down Bella's naked body.

She shifted closer to him, her fingers twining in his, as if she could hide behind him. It grated on Alex that he couldn't provide the comfort or protection that she truly needed. He promised himself that after they escaped, once they were safe, he was going to make sure never to be in a position where he couldn't take care of her, ever again.

"Ah, Pet and Toy are here," the Wolf said, reaching down to stroke Cora's hair. She released his cock from her mouth, leaving it slick and shiny as she wrapped her hand around it, slowly pumping the long shaft as she looked over at them. The eagerness in her eyes made Alex shiver. Would he be able to distract her from Bella again? Some part of him hoped that the Wolf might help keep Cora from unleashing her more sadistic tendencies on Bella, but the Wolf had already proved himself unreliable when it came to shielding either of them. Sometimes he did, sometimes he didn't, and they never knew which it was going to be.

"Lovely," Cora purred. "We've so been looking forward to playing with you again, haven't we Trace?" She shot a sidelong look at the man beside them, who immediately nodded his head. It suddenly occurred to Alex that Trace was looking somehow submissive, standing there, waiting for a word from his mistress. Perhaps she was his mistress in more than just employment. "You've taken Toy's collar off?"

"He'll behave," the Wolf said idly, his hand stroking down her body as she continued to fist his cock. "Won't you, Toy?" His green eyes gleamed, as if he knew something that Alex didn't. Alex nodded, because he would behave today. He didn't want to risk getting separated from Bella, not now that they'd recovered their lost memories and had a real chance at escape.

"Let's string Toy up on the bed so he can watch us play with the pretty Pet," Cora said, her eyes sparkling maliciously. She smiled at Trace. "You do want to play with the pretty Pet, don't you darling?"

"Yes Ma'am," Trace said, his deep voice eager.

Alex growled again, but he didn't resist as the soldiers led him over to the bed.

14

Trying to hide behind the soldiers was silly and useless, but Bella couldn't seem to stop herself. No one was touching her, or forcing her to move closer to the bed with them, but somehow she felt more exposed and vulnerable by herself, with no one else next to her. The Wolf, Cora and Trace all watched her as she trailed along behind Alex, shifting back and forth on her feet as the soldiers secured him to the large bed, his hands to the top of the frame, his legs to the bottom.

Then the soldiers left, as the Wolf removed Cora's hand from his cock and rolled off the bed. He came over, and Bella trembled as he approached, her head tipping back to look at him. Out of the corner of her eye, she could see Alex straining to look behind him— maybe just so that he didn't have to look at Cora, maybe so that he could see what the Wolf was doing to her.

"Pretty Pet," the Wolf said, putting two fingers under her chin and keeping her head tilted back. Those piercing green eyes were almost frightening right now, the intensity of his gaze heightening her anxiety. "You were so good this morning, weren't you?"

Bella's trembling increased, her breath stuttering as she realized that he *had* to be referring to the fact that she'd remembered the passageway but hadn't tried to escape.

The Wolf knew.

His mouth lowered, his kiss almost gentle, and she parted her lips for him as his tongue delved in. It was the kiss of a lover, and it shocked her, nearly as much as discovering that he knew she'd remembered.

"You're going to be rewarded now. Get on the bed."

Cora was on the bed, so Bella couldn't figure how he thought that would be a reward. Still trembling, she obeyed.

"Trace has been so looking forward to playing with you," the older woman said as Bella crawled onto the bed beside her. "I could almost be jealous. Except, of course, that I have been as well. Lay on your back and spread your legs. We want to see your pretty pink pussy. I bet Toy does too."

They'd placed Alex at the foot of the bed, so she looked at him, gaining what strength she could from his gaze, as she laid back and obediently spread her legs. It was heartening to see the reluctant excitement in Alex's eyes; knowing that he didn't want to be turned on, but that he couldn't help but be aroused by her.

In his position, he would have the perfect view of her pussy as the pink folds spread, exposed and vulnerable. Bella shivered as the Wolf stepped up behind him and began running his hands up and down Alex's sides, making him tense and jerk against his restraints. Already Alex's cock was beginning to harden.

Laying down next to Bella, facing her, Cora gave Trace a lazy glance over her shoulder. "Come onto the bed, darling, I want to see you touch her."

The big, bald man eagerly climbed onto the bed, kneeling between Bella's legs as his hands came down on her breasts. Cora didn't touch Bella, she just watched as Trace's huge hands engulfed her pale flesh, his fingers immediately seeking out her sensitive nipples, his large body looming over hers.

This entire situation was confusing her; she didn't know what to think or what was going on. She'd expected to be punished for recovering her memories, then the Wolf said this was a reward, but Cora had proven herself to be a cruel sadist, and yet Trace had been almost kind to Bella before...

And now his hands and mouth were bringing her nothing but pure pleasure. He didn't bite or squeeze too hard, but he nibbled and nipped, his tongue flicking over the hard little buds which were beginning to ache, and he squeezed and kneaded her breasts just firmly enough to make her moan.

She dug her fingers into the mattress as her back arched slightly, thrusting her breasts up at Trace. The hot sucking of his mouth was sending flashes of pleasure straight down to her pussy, making her clench in time with his suckling as her pussy slicked. Cora was beside them, watching, her eyes practically glowing, and Bella realized that the woman was getting off on controlling Trace as he touched Bella.

Although she couldn't see him, with Trace's big body in the way, Bella heard Alex groan and wondered what the Wolf was doing to him. She didn't have to wait too long to find out.

"Her nipples are sensitive, aren't they? Are you enjoying Trace, Pet? He's very talented with his mouth. Trace, show Pet how good you are with your tongue, I want to see you lick her pussy."

Leveraging himself downward, Trace licked his way down Bella's stomach, making her quiver as he came closer and closer to her swollen folds. She was aroused; she couldn't help it... he really was good with his mouth and being the center of attention like this was arousing her even though she didn't want it to. As Trace moved, she was finally able to see Alex, his frowning expression as if he was fighting against something. The Wolf was practically wrapped around him, pressed up against his back, arms around him, one hand slowly pumping Alex's cock while the other gripped his balls, rolling them firmly back and forth in his palm. It looked like Alex was caught in exquisite pain.

———

It felt like his jaw might break, he was grinding down on his teeth so hard. The Wolf's touch was torturous. One hand was pumping his cock with long, slow strokes, the Wolf's thumb brushing over Alex's sensitive head every time it reached the end of his shaft. The other had pulled Alex's balls down in his sack, stretching the loose skin, and he was rolling the tender nuts back and forth in a way that bordered on being breathtakingly painful. The mix of sensations was making Alex lightheaded.

And all the while, he was having to watch Bella writhe and arch as Trace lowered his head between her thighs. Alex had to admit that there was something erotically charged about it, even though he hated seeing another man pleasuring Bella.

Trace, unlike the Wolf or his men, was being almost sweet with her. Despite the fact that he was taking orders from Cora, Alex could tell that Bella was responding to everything that Trace was doing to her. She was gorgeous in her passion, and that was part of what was keeping his own cock rigidly hard in the Wolf's hand.

Cora reached out and pinched one of Bella's nipples, hard, making her shriek as her body arched, pressing her pussy even more firmly against Trace's mouth. Immediately, Bella reached up, trying to dislodge the other woman's fingers from the sensitive bud. Laughing, the older woman grabbed Bella's wrists and held them above Bella's head. Moving upward on the bed, Cora knelt over Bella's face, pressing Bella's arms into the bed with her legs, her pussy inches from Bella's face.

Looking up at Alex, Cora smiled sadistically as she reached down to pinch Bella's sensitive nipples again. "Like what you see, Toy? She's so responsive, isn't she? I bet you like to play with her too... I can see how much you're enjoying watching us play with her."

A slightly muffled shriek emerged from between Cora's legs as she twisted the tender buds of Bella's nipples, making Bella writhe as she tried to shake the other woman off of her. Blood surged in Alex's cock, a rush of anger that somehow transmuted into arousal as the Wolf gripped his shaft more tightly. Alex growled, and the frame of the bed shook with his body's tremors.

Ignoring him, Cora continued to pull and twist Bella's nipples, avidly watching Trace's efforts to pleasure their captive. Bella whimpered and moaned, pinned down by Cora's legs and Trace's hands, unable to stop both the pleasure and the pain. As the Wolf's hand tightened around Alex's cock, he could only groan as he watched, struggling against his own arousal even as pre-cum began to leak from the head of his cock, thanks to the Wolf's slow, steady strokes.

Behind him, Alex could feel the bulge of the Wolf's erection pressing against his ass, rubbing across his cheeks, only a thin barrier of fabric separating them.

The bowing of Bella's body said that she was approaching orgasm, despite Cora's rough handling of her nipples. Or maybe because of it. The tiny nubs were dark pink from their abuse, but Bella was still lifting her hips and rubbing her pussy against Trace's tongue.

"Fuck her now, darling," Cora said, looking even more excited. "She's ready for it, aren't you, Pet?" She pinched and tugged on Bella's nipples, making her squeal.

The Wolf's breath was coming fast and hot on the back of Alex's neck; he was getting turned on by watching, although his strokes of Alex's cock were just as infuriatingly steady and slow as ever. The need to come was building, but Alex would never get there the way the Wolf was jacking him off. The Wolf's cock nestled between Alex's ass cheeks, holding him firmly in place against the bed as they watched Trace slide up Bella's body, hooking her legs over his arms and spreading her wide.

———

Bella had closed her eyes to shut out the sight of Cora's pussy hovering over her. It was almost a threatening sight because she didn't know when those swollen folds would descend, or how she would breathe once they did. Although, the sadistic woman seemed far more interested in torturing Bella's nipples at the moment, the perfume of her arousal filling Bella's nose as the pain in her nipples increased.

She couldn't stop the whimpers or squeals that escaped as Cora tortured her tits, even knowing that they only spurred the other woman on. But those sounds were also interspersed with moans as Trace's tongue explored her pussy, licking his way up and down her slit eagerly, and tracing erotic circles around her clit. The man was incredible at eating pussy, teasing her folds, building her arousal higher and higher so that the hot flashes of pain from her nipples swirled into the pleasure.

Cora was saying something, although Bella couldn't hear the words, with Cora's thighs and pussy covering her head, but she could feel Trace moving up her body. She moaned, breathing in the musky scent of Cora's cunt, feeling Trace's cock pressing against her own pussy. The pressure was immense, and she ached as her pussy stretched open for his girth. Bella tried to squirm away, but she couldn't because of the way they were holding her in place.

Then Cora began to shift back, although she kept her weight on Bella's wrists, and Bella opened her eyes. Cora had moved back so that Trace could sink his cock more fully into Bella's pussy. The huge man leaned over her, his eyes practically glowing, as he thrust forward. Bella screamed in pained ecstasy as her pussy was completely impaled upon his shaft. He was huge, the end of his cock pressing against her cervix, and she whimpered as he circled his hips, rubbing his body against her swollen folds and clit, rubbing his cockhead against her womb.

"Fuck yes... use that pretty pink pussy," Cora said, her hands coming down to rest on Bella's shoulders.

Because Trace was so tall, the way he was positioned over Bella prevented Cora from reaching Bella's nipples without getting in the way of his deep thrusts. But she held Bella down, keeping her completely immobile as Trace groaned with pleasure, thrusting hard and fast, splitting Bella's pussy open on his thick cock.

The orgasm that she'd almost reached when he'd been suckling on her hovered just out of reach as her body slowly adjusted to the huge cock pounding into her. The friction and strain made her pussy burn, even as clit throbbed with every smacking slap of Trace's body against hers.

"Lean back," she heard Cora order him.

Lifting Bella's legs even higher, Trace obeyed his commander, bringing his knees under Bella's thighs as he sat up, looking down at Bella's body and her swollen pink pussy wrapped around his thick cock. Feeling almost dizzy, Bella looked down too, shocked at how strangely erotic it was to see him buried inside of her, Alex and the Wolf watching over his shoulder.

Then Cora's hands came down on her breasts again, squeezing the soft mounds hard, although she left Bella's nipples alone for the moment. Still, her fingers dug into Bella's flesh painfully, making her squirm and tighten around Trace's cock. He groaned with pleasure even as Bella whimpered in pain, her inner muscles grasping his shaft as he moved within her, making her burn even more, inside and out.

"Fuck her hard."

As if he hadn't been already!

Bella cried out as Trace's large hands gripped her hips and he began to pound into her mercilessly. Every thrust had his cock dragging over her g-spot, and a different kind of fire was beginning to burn inside of her, warring with and blending with the more painful flames. Bella tried to arch as Cora's fingers tugged at her nipples, but she couldn't move very much, and doing so just made Trace's cock feel like it was sliding even deeper inside of her.

Her orgasm rocketed through her, unexpectedly, as Trace suddenly changed tempo, pressing his body against her clit and rocking before dragging his cock out again. The swollen nub exploded with the stimulation, making her pussy convulse and flutter over the length of his dick as she screamed out her climax. The pressure on her nipples increased and she sobbed as Trace continued to fuck her just as hard, making sure to press against her clit every time, drowning her in waves of ecstasy so intense that she could barely breathe.

His cock expanded and throbbed, heat filling her belly as he pumped jets of cum deep inside of her. The convulsions of her cunt milked him, pulling at his cock, and the rest of her body went limp as the last shudders of her orgasm were wrung from her. Her pussy felt tingly and exquisitely sensitive, her muscles clenching with every brush of his skin against hers.

As Cora lifted herself up and away, it didn't even matter that she wasn't holding Bella down anymore, because Bella was too wrung out to even squirm.

15

"Bring Toy to the bed," Cora said.

Alex couldn't help but groan as the Wolf released his cock; he hadn't been far from coming, even with the Wolf's slow strokes. His balls ached, the painful need reaching up his spine and spreading throughout his lower back as his cock bobbed in the air while the Wolf undid his restraints. On the bed, Trace was pulling Bella off to the side, tucking her into his body so that her back was pressed against his front, facing where Cora was sitting and waiting. Bella looked utterly languid, her eyelids half-mast, and she didn't even flinch as Trace fondled her breast. Between her legs, her pussy was dark pink and swollen-looking from his rough fucking, cum starting to make the tops of her thighs shiny as it seeped from her pussy.

Taking down Alex's arms, the Wolf put his hand on the back of Alex's neck, steering him to the bed. Cora moved to the side as Alex was turned and pushed down, landing on his back. Immediately, she climbed on top of him, straddling him, and his cock strained upward toward her pussy, his body desperately eager to be buried in something.

Gripping him at the base, Cora squeezed tightly enough to make him wince with pain and try to reach down and stop her, but she was already lowering herself onto him. His body jerked as the combination of pain and pleasure swept through him and scrambled his brain. Her pussy was soaking wet from torturing Bella and watching her with Trace, liquid heat running down his cock in advance of her body as her juices dripped down his shaft.

"Ooooh yes,", she moaned as she slid down. Alex had to grit his teeth against voicing a similar sentiment of pleasure. His body might not care whose pussy was engulfing his dick, but he did.

Cora leaned forward, grabbing his hands and pushing them down by his head as she started to move up and down on top of him, riding him. Although he was stronger than her, she had the leverage advantage and he didn't bother to fight her, knowing it was useless anyway. She tossed a look over her shoulder at the Wolf, and Alex felt the bed shift between his legs as the Wolf joined them.

He could actually feel it when the Wolf slid his finger into Cora's ass. The thin wall between her holes made it seem as though the Wolf was stroking the length of Alex's cock, while it was buried inside of Cora. She tightened around Alex, voicing her pleasure. When he added a second finger, it made her pussy feel even tighter around Alex's cock.

She was moving slowly on top of him, her inner muscles gripping him so tightly it was almost painful, keeping him from being able to come because the stimulation just wasn't quite enough. Alex was just her sex toy, there for her pleasure, while she and the Wolf took theirs together. Turning his head, he could see Bella and Trace watching. The big man had one hand cupping Bella's breast, gently rolling her nipple between his fingers. Despite the abuse the stiff little bud had taken from Cora, it looked like Bella was becoming aroused again.

Alex closed his eyes, shutting out the sight, just as he felt the Wolf's cock begin to slide into Cora's ass. She moaned and writhed on top of him, her pussy clenching, as she was filled in both holes. He clenched his jaw, straining to come and get this over with, but she held so still on top of him as the Wolf worked his way into her ass, that Alex couldn't get off.

Her hole tightened around him, not because she was clenching, but because there was less space in her body as she was filled. Cora was trembling between them, moaning ecstatically, her nails digging into the backs of Alex's hands as she squirmed on top of him.

"Good girl," the Wolf said, rocking her gently on top of Alex. He used the same tone he often did with Bella, but Cora's eyes snapped open and flashed with annoyance.

"Fuck me," she rasped, pushing back against both of the men, demanding in a way that Bella would never have been. She and the Wolf were two dominants, fighting each other, and using the others to sate their need for control. No wonder they loved the fight with Alex, since they could never win the tussle with each other. They needed each other for an ally, but he was just collateral.

They began to move on top of him, and Alex groaned, straining beneath them as Cora's pussy throbbed around his cock. He could feel the slide of the Wolf's dick in and out of her ass, rubbing against his as they battled for space inside of her body. Cora moaned happily as they fucked her, moving up and down on Alex's cock, lifting her ass as the Wolf thrust in, rubbing her pussy folds and clit against Alex's groin, and absorbing every last bit of pleasure that she could.

He could feel his own orgasm rising as his over-worked cock was finally getting the stimulation it needed. The constant toying of the Wolf and Cora had had him on edge for what felt like forever, and the resulting buildup was more than painful; it felt like his cock was about to burst open.

The ecstasy was red-hot, burning through him, as his cum seemed to boil up out of his balls. It felt like the muscles in his back were aching as he emptied, Cora's tight pussy literally squeezing the orgasm out of him as she spasmed and clenched. But it didn't end there; she kept moving, not caring that he'd already come, squeezing his cock even after it was empty and trying to soften. The relief edged into pain, stabbing into his groin as the sensation of climaxing continued, intensifying far beyond what was pleasurable as his sensitized dick was massaged and squeezed. He only softened to about half-mast, unable to escape the vise of Cora's cunt, still feeling the Wolf's cock rubbing against him inside of her.

He groaned, trying to push her up and off of him, but he was too drained and the combination of her weight and the Wolf's was too heavy. The constant movements against his groin, the way her pussy squeezed him, made the blood begin to return to his cock, begin to fill it again, at least enough to make her writhe with pleasure.

Bella whimpered as Trace's fingers, coated with their combined juices, pushed into her ass from behind. His breath was hot on the back of her neck, excited from watching the threesome beside them. Even Bella had to admit—visually, it was hot. But she could tell from the way Alex was gritting his teeth, the way his muscles were straining, that it had ceased to be pleasurable for him. He'd already come, but Cora continued to ride him. Bella hadn't even known that was possible.

And now Trace was aroused again, she could feel his hard cock pressing into the soft cheeks of her ass as he fingered her anus, readying the tight hole. Even though she'd become used to having her asshole used, Bella still struggled with the initial stretch and burning discomfort. Especially when his fingers were replaced but the much thicker, longer girth of his cock, while she was being forced to watch Alex being abused by Cora and the Wolf.

She panted as Trace slid into her from behind, his hand back on her breast, toying with her sore nipple, as he filled her backside. The tiny whimpers and squirming movements she made were completely drowned out by the Wolf and Cora's much louder moans, Alex's pained grunts, and the wet slap of bodies coming from the other side of the bed.

It felt like her ass was being strained by the size of Trace's cock, and she whimpered as he dragged himself back out over what felt like raw exposed nerve endings. He shifted slightly, pushing her farther onto her stomach, her face turned to the side to watch Alex, Cora and the Wolf, so that he could go deeper, thrust harder into her vulnerable asshole.

"Fuck..." he murmured into her ear as his hand slid down to her pussy, fingers rubbing over her swollen clit and making her whimper as her body spasmed with renewed pleasure. His caresses assuaged some of the discomfort he was causing with his cock, mingling the pleasure and pain together in an erotic symphony that made her entire body tingle.

She dug her fingers into the sheets beneath her, gasping, as Trace began to rock faster, thrusting deeply into her asshole as his fingers rolled around her sensitive clit. Her body bucked, impaling herself further onto his cock, meeting his thrusts, as he skillfully built her orgasm back up.

Sudden warmth covered her fingers and she opened her eyes to see Alex staring back at her, his hand over hers. They clasped each other's hands, coming together in a moment of unity, despite what was happening to them. The grim, pained expression on Alex's face was mingled with growing lust, and she knew that they were both caught in the same web of sensory contradictions.

Trace seemed as determined to pleasure her as he was himself, even though she struggled against it. Somehow, holding Alex's hand only made it harder for her to resist the waves of pleasure that were now rippling through her, the hot lances of rapture that followed Trace's every thrust. Her ass had adjusted, and the burning friction of his cock as it plunged in and out of her body made her cry out as the pathway to her orgasm spiraled higher.

She screamed when it broke over her, washing through her body and burning her from the inside out. Her hand tightened on Alex's as Trace pistoned in and out of her, fucking her ass with long hard strokes as she convulsed around him. The stabbing motion of his cock penetrated deep as he swelled larger, before spurting his sticky, warm cum into her channel.

Alex's fingers wrapped more tightly around hers a few moments later, and she knew that he was coming again as well, while Cora and the Wolf enjoyed their own passionate culmination.

————

The room they were returned to was not their own. It had the exact same layout as their previous room, but when Bella awoke, wrapped up in Alex's arms, and looked at the walls, there were no sigils. Her body ached, especially her pussy and ass, the lingering sensations alerting her to the lack of healing cream. Maybe that was good though; the Wolf wasn't trying to make sure that she and Alex were ready for another go-round.

Being healed quickly usually meant being used quickly again too.

"Alex," she whispered, stroking his arm to wake him up as she craned her neck around, checking the other walls and confirming her suspicions.

He came awake fast, jolting her out of his arms as he sat up, alert and defensive. After a quick sweep of his gaze around the room, once he saw that they were alone, he relaxed. "What? What's wrong?"

Bella pointed at the empty walls. "They moved us..."

Which meant that they couldn't get out. There was no escape. Alex's features hardened and then shifted into confusion.

"Why move us?" he murmured. "Why not just make us forget again?"

"Maybe because it didn't work so well last time?"

"It worked well enough for a while," he countered, rubbing his hands over his face.

Bella shifted closer to him on the bed, seeking comfort. She really hated when they didn't know what was going on.

Immediately, Alex put his arm around her and snuggled her in close, allowing her to relax as she sank into the comfort of his embrace. "What are they up to?"

The question was rhetorical, because neither of them had any answers.

16

Trish didn't know what to think. Glancing at the big man seated next to her in the back seat, his hand wrapped firmly around hers, she felt frightened. She hadn't been told anything, had no idea what was going on, all she knew was that she was leaving the compound for the first time since she'd been taken.

And she didn't want to.

It was a startling and fairly frightening realization. But she felt safe in the compound. Everyone watched out for her, even when Jordan wasn't around. Everyone cared for her. She had actual friends, who waved to her in the hallway, chatted with her at mealtime, and never once looked at her with pity because she was an orphan or contempt because she wasn't rich. They all came from different places, different backgrounds, and yet they came together and none of that mattered. It was completely different from the way she'd grown up on the Moon, where background and family status were all that mattered and everyone was judged by that. Even winning a scholarship to Earth had been seen as a reason for derision, because anyone who mattered wouldn't need such a thing.

She told herself that she'd gotten used to the demands that Jordan put on her body, the pain and pleasure, the punishment and rewards, but the truth was, she'd started to like it.

Leaving the compound made her start to worry that this time in her life was over, even though Jordan hadn't said so. He was still holding her hand as the hover-car began to move, although he was talking on his earpiece to someone in one of the other cars. Looking around, Trish could see that there were six other cars, completely filled with the Wolf's soldiers just like this one, heading out with them. She couldn't imagine Jordan taking her on a dangerous outing... but would he take this many people if he was going to get rid of her somehow?

The buildings on Earth passed by the window; the compound was larger than it looked from the inside when she peeked back at it. It was well hidden among plenty of other buildings with similar design. Surely they couldn't all be harboring criminals...

Next to her, Jordan pressed a finger to his earpiece. "Is everything in place? Good, we're on our way for pickup... any concerns we should be aware of?" He snorted derisively at whatever the other person responded. "I mean real concerns. Okay, good. We'll be there soon."

He pressed the earpiece again, turning off the call, and then his hand came down on Trish's thigh, gripping her with his fingers as he turned his head to look down at her. She froze, only now realizing that she'd been squirming on the seat next to him, restless with all the anxious energy swirling around inside of her. The sensation of his hot palm against her thigh made her entire body quiver and then still, waiting to see what he would do next.

"Calm down, baby," he said softly, giving her thigh a reassuring squeeze. "Nothing bad is going to happen to you."

Almost immediately, she felt calmer. She trusted Jordan in that. If he said nothing bad was going to happen to her, she believed him.

"Where are we going?" she whispered, her gaze sliding across to the other soldiers in the car's interior. They weren't paying any attention to her and Jordan, but she never knew how he was going to take it when she questioned him in front of others.

"I have to make a pickup for the Wolf," he said amiably, his fingers beginning to draw up her skirt so that he could stroke the soft inside of her thigh. Trish knew better than to try and stop him or to press her legs together, even though she hated being exposed in front of the other soldiers. They would never touch, but they would look, and that was bad enough. It was another demonstration of Jordan's domination, over her and over the soldiers.

Her nipples hardened as his hand slid deeper between her legs, his fingers searching out the lips of her pussy.

"Spread," he ordered, giving her a warning look not to argue.

Trish bit her lower lip as she spread her legs, wishing that her skirt would fall into place to cover her, but instead it just moved up her thighs and showed off more of her body. Jordan's hand would cover her pussy though. His fingers slid into her folds, and he smiled as he found them already wet.

The slow exploration his fingers were making of her

pussy wasn't going to get her off any time soon, it was just going to torment her as they drove. She shivered, keeping her hands by her sides, her body tingling and coming alive as he teased at her sensitive folds, slipping just the tip of a finger inside of her and then withdrawing it again. Cream was spread up to her clit, wetting the tiny nub and making it slick and hard under his ministrations.

She was panting and achy when he suddenly stopped, and she moaned in disappointment. With a little laugh, he brought his soaked fingers up to her lips and pressed them in, making her clean off her own juices.

The man had timed it perfectly. The hover-car landed just as she finished, leaving her unsatisfied, needy, and with the taste of sex on her tongue. But she didn't protest as Jordan helped her out of the car.

Blinking, she realized that she recognized where they were; it was a museum. One that she'd visited before she'd been taken. Jordan pulled her inside, her hand firmly clasped in his. The Wolf's soldiers spread out through the crowd walking up the steps, and she realized that only a few of them were in uniform, mostly the ones that had ridden in the same car with her and Jordan. The rest were dressed just like anyone else. So was Jordan, although anyone who thought he was just a regular guy —at his height, with his muscles, and his fluid way of moving—was an idiot. With one heavy arm slung around Trish's shoulders, keeping her pressed close by his side, he moved them into the museum.

It didn't take her more than a few minutes to realize that Jordan wasn't actually looking at any of the exhibits, although he did stop in front of several of them, taking a minute before moving on. Trish looked at the first few, but as she realized he had some destination, some goal, in mind, she found herself becoming too nervous to pay attention. Instead, her gaze began to dart around the room, her weight shifting restlessly as she wondered what he was looking for.

"Stay still and look at the painting," Jordan murmured in her ear, leaning down as if making some kind of innocuous comment about the restored Impressionist painting they were currently standing in front of. "Or I'll spank you the entire ride home."

Immediately, Trish focused in on the painting. It was beautiful, and she'd always loved old Earth art, so it should have been more than enough to hold her attention, but she found herself staring at it without really seeing it. She didn't doubt that Jordan would spank her, the entire ride, which had taken about fifteen minutes, and she really didn't want that. But at least now she knew what he'd brought her for. To help him blend in.

Someone like Jordan would always be noticed. He was too big, too lethal, for people to ignore. But pair him with a sweet-looking young woman like Trish, and he no longer stood out quite so much. People glanced and saw a smaller female with a large, protective man, a possessive one by his stance and the way he was constantly looking around at everyone. They would be judged as a couple, and he would immediately be seen as less threatening because of her presence. Everyone would assume that he was there because his girlfriend wanted to look at culture; they would accept his distraction and preoccupation as long as they saw her focusing on the exhibits.

She understood the psychological and sociological ramifications of her presence quite clearly. After all, she'd always been a good student. Most people wouldn't even realize how she was being used, they wouldn't actually think through why they weren't intimidated by him, or why they found him non-threatening after seeing her, they would just react.

Slowly they moved deeper into the museum, Jordan directing where they went. Sometimes she glimpsed other members of his team, sometimes it seemed like they were completely alone. The further into the building they went, the more tense she became. To her dismay, he started adding minutes to a tally. Every time he felt she wasn't playing her part, he added another minute that he would be spanking her on the ride home.

By the time they reached the room filled with artifacts of the Ancient Egyptians, Trish was up to seven minutes. She felt Jordan tense beside her, his focus on the end of the room. Pretending to study the headdress in front of her—which, the sign said, was actually a reproduction, as the original was too old and delicate to have out on the museum floor—she dared to look down the long length of the room. There was a group of people down there, a couple and what looked like several bodyguards around them.

The bodyguards weren't even trying to blend in. They were heavily muscled and wore athletic clothing, with suspicious bulges on their hips that were probably guns which had been covered up by the sashes around their waist. The couple must be from very prominent Moon families. Trish hadn't heard of anyone who could afford the bodyguards being attacked; only the wealthiest and most powerful could afford such men, and they were never needed as anything more than a deterrent.

Her heart began to pound as one of Jordan's soldiers

—a ferociously deadly woman named Zadia—came up beside them. Zadia frightened Trish. The woman reminded her of Cora. Trish had seen the soldiers spar and she knew that if Zadia joined the mats, there was never any other winner. Only Jordan could go toe to toe with her, and even he could only beat her about half the time. He'd once told Trish that Zadia was going to be his replacement one day, as she was younger than him and soon even he wouldn't be able to defeat her as she grew in strength and skill.

"Everyone's in position," Zadia murmured, her dark black eyes focused on the headdress. She was dressed like a civilian, blending in much better than Jordan did, with her long dark hair and tanned skin. Small, but deadly. No one was frightened of Zadia when they first looked at her, unlike Jordan.

"Good. Watch over Trish."

Surprised, Trish didn't even protest as he moved away. Not that it would have done any good. Jordan began walking, nonchalantly, toward the guarded couple at the back of the room. Trish's eyes widened as she real-ized that she recognized every single person in the room. The couple and their guards were completely surrounded by the Wolf's soldiers. How had they managed to clear an entire museum room of everyone else?

"What's happening?" she whispered. Zadia hushed her, pulling Trish back toward the entrance to the room, keeping an eye out on the soldiers who were moving in the opposite direction—toward the couple. Were they the Wolf's next targets? Were Alex and Bella going to be returned to the Moon?

But everyone knew the Wolf only took stragglers, those who were dumb enough —or overly confident enough—to venture out on their own. Not couples in the middle of a museum, in the middle of the afternoon, not people who were actually guarded. Whatever was happening, it was more important than the usual kidnapping. She eyed Zadia, keeping her voice to a whisper. "Why aren't you down there with them? Don't you want to be a part of what's happening?"

"Shows what you know," Zadia whispered back harshly. Her dark eyes glinted with smugness. "I was given the more important assignment."

Trish.

She was the more important assignment?

Shouts echoed through the room and Trish immediately turned to see what was going on. Fighting—the soldiers swarming the bodyguards, who were fighting back. Screams—the woman, clinging to the man beside her and hampering him from any kind of defense he might have been able to put up. Jordan was next to them, reaching for them... and then a hand wrapped around Trish's wrist and pulled.

She yelped as Zadia dragged her out of the room.

"Come on," the other woman ordered. "We're going this way."

"Why?" Trish asked, digging in her heels. She could see people already moving toward the Egyptian hall, most of them curious onlookers, a few of them that looked like security guards of some kind.

"In case they get caught. My job is to get you to the rendezvous. From a different direction. Now come on."

There was no way Trish could shake off Zadia's grip as the other woman waved frantically at the approaching museum guards.

"They have guns!" Zadia yelled, sounding completely panicked as she pulled Trish right by them.

Immediately the guards slowed down, approaching the room more cautiously even though the shouting had stopped. They ignored Zadia and Trish completely, which had probably been the goal from the beginning. Trish followed Zadia, knowing that it was useless to try and do anything else. She could probably escape right now, quite easily, but to what? If her scholarship hadn't already been given away, she doubted that the sponsors would be pleased to see her, regardless. No one had seemed to care enough to report her missing to the media. She'd seen the videos. Only Alex and Bella had gotten any coverage.

And she wanted to know that Jordan was okay. Half of the fear pounding through her heart right now wasn't for herself, but because she was worried that he'd be caught or hurt. Stupid, because she knew that he was kidnapping or maybe even murdering someone else right now, but there it was. All she could think about was what might be happening in that other room. Sure, Zadia's warning about guns had slowed down the guard, but wouldn't it also make them more likely to use deadly force?

The fact that Jordan had separated himself from her, putting Zadia in charge of her safety, also said that he wasn't entirely confident in the smoothness of whatever plan he'd enacted. If he'd been sure of himself, he would have kept Trish by his side. She knew that much, because he rarely let her go anywhere without him.

People were already panicking all around them as alarms began blaring, blending her and Zadia into the crowd as they rushed toward the exit. The second they got outside, Zadia turned, giving Trish no choice but to follow along behind her. She was sure that she was going to have red marks on her wrist from Zadia's unrelenting grip. They hurried down the street, which was boiling over with people going in all directions, staring at the museum as the alarm was audible even from the outside of the building.

Three blocks away, Zadia pulled Trish to a long line of hover-cars, opening the door to the third one from the front and shoving Trish in. She fell to the floor of the car in a heap as the door slammed behind her. All she could see were multiple boots surrounding her.

"Careful baby girl," Jordan's deep voice murmured, sounding amused.

Trish relaxed as he picked her up and pulled her onto his lap. Unlike her, Jordan wasn't even breathing hard, he looked as if he'd just gone for a stroll. Except for the triumphant expression on his face. His eyes were practically glowing.

"Are you all right?"

"Yes," she said, although her hand automatically went to her wrist, which was bit sore.

Immediately Jordan's focus changed, and he took her hand, lifting it so that he could inspect her wrist. It only took him a moment to nod, as if confirming her declaration.

"Good, then we can get on with your punishment."

"Wait!" Trish squealed as she was flipped over his knee into an all-too-familiar position, and her skirt was drawn up. She'd almost forgotten his threat from the museum.

"You earned seven minutes, sweetheart, starting now."

SMACK! SMACK! SMACK!

The slaps to her ass weren't particularly hard, but Trish moaned anyway, knowing that after seven minutes they were going still going to feel like fire. Each measured blow was firmly delivered, marching down one cheek and up the other from the top curve of her ass to her sit-spot. The first three repetitions stung, but she didn't really start to squirm and whimper until the fourth. By then, her ass was a bright-pink color, her skin warmed up and sensitive, and each firm smack felt like a little flame licking at her bottom.

"That's one minute."

Grabbing onto the seat, Trish buried her face in it, trying to stifle her cries, knowing that it was only going to get worse over the next six minutes. Jordan didn't vary the intensity of his blows at all, but that's not how it felt. By the time he called out three minutes, Trish was openly crying, wriggling to try and escape the hard smacks, pinned in place by Jordan's hand.

Halfway through that minute, he picked her up and turned her over his lap the other way, joking to the soldiers with them that his hand was getting tired. Trish wanted to kick him. Then it started up again, only this time with his other hand, and the difference was definitely discernible to her poor cheeks. Trish howled.

The worst part was, despite the chuckling soldiers, despite the flaming pain, between her legs she knew that she was slick and creamy with arousal. Her mound pressed against Jordan's thigh, and as much as her bottom was wagging to try and ease the sting, she was also trying to rub herself against the hard muscle of his leg. The spanking might be humiliating, it might feel like her ass was on fire, but her pussy didn't care. It just got wetter and wetter even as she cried out with pain.

"Last minute."

She shrieked as Jordan's hand came down, not on her ass, but between her legs, firmly smacking her swollen pussy lips. They plumped up even more under the unexpected assault. Pleasure flashed through her, edged with pain, and she shuddered and tried to close her legs. Jordan smacked her sit-spots, which were already red-hot and painfully throbbing, and she sobbed as she forced her legs apart again.

The muted smacks landed on wet flesh as she bucked on his lap, throbbing inside and outside as he spanked her pussy, the tips of his fingers occasionally catching her clit and causing the little nubbin to puff up even further. Oh god... she couldn't come—wouldn't come—while he spanked her pussy... she wouldn't!

"Good girl," Jordan murmured, and his hand came down to rest on her sensitive mound, fingers massaging the swollen, heated flesh, stroking away the sting. Trish clenched, empty and grasping at nothing, but trying all the same.

He rubbed his hand over her bottom, making her gasp as sensations flared, coming back to life. As he'd spanked her pussy, she'd almost forgotten how much her ass hurt.

Then he was pushing her onto her knees, and Trish knew what came next. One hand slid into her hair while the other undid the front of his pants, and his cock sprung out, erect and ready.

"Play with yourself," he ordered her, as he pulled her head down, pushing her lips over the plump head of his dick. "If you can't make yourself come before we arrive, you'll have to wait until this evening."

As she opened her mouth to take him inside, her

tongue flicking the sweet drop of liquid from his tip, his free hand cupped her breast and pinched the nipple, rolling it between his fingers.

Need shuddered through her, even as her lower body throbbed from the spanking. She pressed her fingers into her pussy, feeling the slick wetness coat her fingers. The musky taste of man filled her mouth as Jordan pushed her head down, forcing himself into her throat. Rubbing her clit, she groaned, her vocal chords fluttering and humming against his cock and he moaned in response, thrusting his hips up and shoving himself across her tongue until her nose pressed against his groin.

He began to thrust in and out, fucking her mouth like it was her pussy. Trish found herself strumming her clit to the same rhythm, the nipple that he was playing with sending sparks of pleasure down to the emptiness inside of her and making her clench and shudder. Her tongue danced along the underside of his cock, stroking its length as it pushed past, his hand in her hair moving her head up and down over his groin.

She let go, giving him complete control over her movements. It was almost mesmerizing to give herself over this way, as if he'd caught her under some kind of spell and she was now his doll, letting him use her to please himself.

The ache between her legs was growing stronger, and she didn't know how much time she had left. Giving up control to Jordan, letting him use her mouth as he wanted, allowed her to focus on her own pleasure. Rubbing her clit hard, she gurgled around his cock as she panted for breath, becoming dizzy as the thick meat filling her throat kept her from getting enough air. It made her entire body tingle, all the sensations from the spanking, the forceful face-fucking, her fingers in her pussy, coming together in a coiled burst between her legs.

Jordan's thrusts were becoming rougher, his hand on her hair tightening, and she knew that they must be getting close to the destination. He would draw his own orgasm out, waiting for the very last minute to finish his own pleasure, and if she didn't keep up with him, she'd miss her chance entirely. She rubbed her clit harder, her hips jerking as her entire body tightened, even her throat, as he thrust deep into her mouth. She couldn't breathe, all she could do was swallow, sucking him dry, drinking his cum as her own ecstasy surged. The throbbing between her legs sent pleasure pulsing through her as she ground her pussy against her hand.

Warmth filled her belly, the taste of cum lingering on her tongue as Jordan withdrew, leaving her panting and gasping for air as the intense orgasm sent the last few quivers of rapture through her. Pulling her up onto his lap, into his arms, Jordan put his hand over hers, pressing it firmly between her legs and making her spasm as ecstasy so intense it hurt ripped through her. Her poor clit cried out for mercy as she writhed, trapped between her body and their hands, as he wrung several more quivering spasms from her.

When he finally stopped, Trish was limp in his arms, completely sated. She barely registered as he covered her up, protective again now that he'd had his release. Leaning her head against his shoulder, she felt the hover-car land. Instead of removing her from his lap, Jordan wrapped his arms around her and carried her out of the car. Trish didn't mind. She'd actually grown to like it when Jordan carried her.

"How are they doing?" he asked one of the soldiers.

Sleepily, Trish turned her head to see who he was talking about. The couple from the museum, unconscious, were being picked up and carried out of one of the other cars. She recognized them from their clothes. The bodyguards, of course, were nowhere to be seen. Then Trish realized that she actually did recognize the couple —and not from the museum. Her jaw dropped.

17

That morning, Bella and Alex weren't taken outdoors, instead they were taken directly to the Wolf's main room. He was sitting behind his desk, but he looked up when they were brought in, a cruel smile sliding over his face.

"Ah, my Pet and Toy," he murmured, his eyes traveling over their naked bodies. Not like he didn't get to see them often enough, but for some reason he was looking at them as though he was enjoying the sight more than usual. "Good, I've been waiting for you."

Not the most comforting words, considering who they were coming from. Alex felt Bella tense beside him, as if she was sure something awful was about to happen to them. Was the Wolf going to make them forget everything now? They didn't know how far back the drug could mess with their memories, but if he did drug all of his captives before returning them to the Moon, then it must be very far back indeed.

The soldiers pushed them forward, and a few minutes later they found themselves in somewhat familiar positions. Bella was on the Wolf's lap, arranged so that her legs were over his and her head was most easily rested on his shoulder. Beside them, on the floor next to the desk, Alex knelt on a cushion. It was the closest he'd ever been to the Wolf's desk while Bella was on the man's lap. Normally he had to watch from afar; now he got a close-up view of the Wolf fondling Bella's breasts and pussy as he worked.

Soldiers came in and out with reports, mostly verbal, during which the Wolf would sit back in his chair, one hand on Bella's breast, pinching her nipple, the other slowly stroking between her legs. Bella kept her face turned away, into the Wolf's shoulder, almost as if she was cuddling against him, but now Alex could see how red her cheeks became, how she was hiding the increased pace of her breathing as the Wolf toyed with her. After their time with him, he knew exactly how to touch Bella to arouse her, and to keep her on edge without giving her satisfaction. Occasionally he'd reach out to run his fingers through Alex's hair. Once he smeared Bella's pussy juices across Alex's lips, as if to show that he hadn't forgotten that Alex was kneeling there.

There was the strangest tension in the air, Alex noticed after a while. The soldiers kept looking toward the door at the end of the room, the big one, as if waiting for something. He felt his own tension beginning to grow. So far today he hadn't seen any sign of Cora or her soldiers.

Finally, the mood in the room shifted, and—almost as if on cue—two soldiers ran up to move the Wolf's desk to the side of the dais, leaving Bella and Alex completely exposed to the room. The Wolf shifted Bella on his lap, so that her back was against the left side of his chest, ostensibly so that she was forced to face the front of the room.

He kept his hand on her breast, but the one that had been between her legs slid over her thigh, wrapping around it almost protectively.

He nodded at a soldier who was standing next to the large door.

Tension in Alex's chest tightened. He hadn't been wearing the collar for days now, the thought of trying to actively attack the Wolf's soldiers had pretty much been dubbed a very bad idea at this point. As soon as the door opened, he almost wished he was still wearing it. At least then he would have an excuse for just standing there, frozen. It felt like he was being sucked down into a whirlpool, like water was rushing past his ears—but even through that, he was so attuned to Bella that he still heard her gasp of recognition.

At the other end of the hall, Ken and Lisa were pushed forward, naked and stumbling. Is that what he and Bella had looked like when they first arrived?

Jordan came in behind them, Trish at his side, his hand wrapped around hers. Alex was surprised to see her shoot a look of distaste at Lisa as the couple was ushered forward.

"I demand you tell me what's happening!" Ken shouted as a soldier came up and grabbed his arm, pulling him down the length of the hall. He was red-faced and practically vibrating with fury, his haughty tones making it clear that he still thought he was in control of the situation. "Do you *know* who my father is?!"

Idiot.

His own response surprised Alex—even though he'd thought Ken was an idiot before, he hadn't expected his own feeling of contempt for his former best friend. Contempt that had nothing to do with the fact that he was a cheater and a shitty friend. No, it was entirely due to looking down at Ken and seeing him as nothing more than a spoiled brat, outraged and unthinking, sure that his money and family's prominence allowed him to talk to others any way that he wanted—even if they'd stripped him down and were half-dragging him through an unknown room.

Lisa seemed a little bit more aware, unlike Ken. She looked up at the dais and seemed to realize immediately where they were. Her lips formed a soft "o" and then her face lit up. The same reaction that Alex had seen from Zander and Maureen, the day captives that the Wolf had procured. Hard on the heels of his contempt for Ken, came a disgust for Lisa. And again, it had nothing to do with her as a cheater. He'd known, from the media vids that the Wolf had allowed them to watch, that she and Ken were grasping at fifteen minutes of fame, but somehow he still wouldn't have thought that she would find herself in the Wolf's hall and be excited about it.

"Gag him."

The Wolf's voice rolled through the room and Alex winced. He'd forgotten about the particular acoustics of this room and the way it could be used to intimidate. It wasn't a trick that the Wolf used on an everyday basis. Ken protested, of course, but the gag was strapped around his head and his hands bound behind his back, to keep him from attempting to remove it, before he could say more than a few words. He didn't try to fight, he just seemed enraged and like he couldn't understand why no one was listening to him.

Alex almost wanted to snort. He might have been a bit of an idiot himself when they were first taken, acting out of instinct and rage, but at least he could feel as though he'd acquitted himself better than Ken currently was. If this was how captives from the Moon normally behaved when taken by the Wolf, he could sympathize more with the Wolf's and the soldiers' dismissive and contemptuous attitude for them. No wonder they'd all been so fascinated by Alex and Bella, and their apparently unusual reactions.

Caressing Bella, the Wolf turned slightly in his chair, to look at Alex. Everything about his demeanor said that he was almost bored by the display being put on in front of him. "So Toy, what do you think of your replacements?"

Both Alex and Bella jerked, as if his words had actually physically hit them.

A chaotic surge of emotions trampled through Alex as the implication of those words hit home.

They were being released...

They could go home.

Ken and Lisa would be left with the Wolf.

They weren't just day captives.

Bella was going to be okay.

What would happen to him and Bella when they returned to the Moon?

Hope, elation, suspicion, concern, relief, all warred inside him as conflicting reactions scattered his wits to the wind. It felt like he'd been punched in the gut; he couldn't even breathe much less respond.

Apparently amused, the Wolf slid his gaze back to Lisa and Ken. Ken was glaring over his gag, his eyes locked onto the Wolf's hand on Bella's breast. Next to him, Lisa was looking back and forth between Alex and the Wolf, completely unconcerned by her nudity, although she was starting to look more confused than excited.

The Wolf looked back at Lisa and Ken, and a small smile curved his lips. Anticipatory. Smug. If Alex hadn't known better, he would have said the Wolf seemed as though he thought Alex and Bella should be pleased by his choice of victims. But why would the Wolf care what his Pet and Toy thought?

Not that Alex even knew what to think. Some part of him felt entirely vindicated to see his cheating ex and back-stabbing former best friend in the same situation that they had, unwittingly, thrust Bella and Alex into with their actions. It had a certain kind of justice to it... but at the same time, there was nothing truly just about the Wolf and his particular use for citizens of the Moon. Alex hadn't thought he would wish his experiences on anyone. Although, if he was going to...

Strangely, he realized he was also slightly disappointed. Not because he wanted to stay, but because he had wanted to escape. The Wolf was going to let him and Bella go, which meant that he wasn't going to be the hero that he'd wanted to be in Bella's eyes. He wasn't going to save her. He'd have nothing to do with it. The Wolf was still controlling everything and it was depressing and frustrating even though the outcome was the same.

Waving his hand, the Wolf looked over to the wall. Bella flinched as she recognized the red hair of Nurse Roche and realized what Lisa and Ken were about to endure. "Nurse Roche, please take Slut and Bitch to be processed. I'd like to spend a little bit of quality time with my Pet and Toy before they go."

18

The Wolf caressed Bella idly as she stared at the man she'd once thought she was in love with. Part of her wanted to laugh at the look of outrage on Ken's face, distorted by the ball-gag that had been forced into his mouth. Next to him, Lisa was staring at Alex, and Bella felt an urge to throw herself off of the Wolf's lap and on top of Alex, to cover him from his ex's eyes. Not that she really thought Alex would be interested in Lisa anymore, but she hated that Lisa could even look at him.

Waving his hand, the Wolf looked over to the wall. Bella flinched as she recognized the red hair of Nurse Roche and realized what Lisa and Ken were about to endure. "Nurse Roche, please take Slut and Bitch to be processed. I'd like to spend a little bit of quality time with my Pet and Toy before they go."

He pinched Bella's nipple as he spoke, making her arch as the tiny bud throbbed with a mix of pain and pleasure. Out of the corner of her eye, she saw Lisa and Ken gape at her, and she closed her eyes so that she didn't have to look. Remembering how the Wolf had played with her and Alex before sending them off for "process-ing," she wasn't sure whether or not she was relieved that he wasn't going to toy with Lisa and Ken. If she'd been forced to watch Alex doing... well, anything, with Lisa, it would have torn her apart.

Slut and Bitch... surprisingly apt names for the two of them. Lisa with her look of excitement when she'd first come in, and Ken, who never stopped bitching.

It was almost strange, actually. Abby had been Slave. Ken and Lisa were Bitch and Slut... When Bella thought about it, Pet and Toy seemed almost affectionate. And the Wolf was actually petting her, stroking her skin in between pinching her nipples. Not that it would keep him from being merciless with her, if he felt like it, but Bella couldn't help but make the comparison in his atti-tude toward Lisa and Ken. Had he chosen them because he thought it would somehow make Alex and Bella happy?

To be honest, Bella wasn't sure how she felt about it.

But she didn't have a whole lot of time to think it through either. Watching them being escorted from the room, Ken still trying to yell behind his gag, and Lisa looking back over her shoulder at both Alex and the Wolf, the Wolf was already sliding his hand between Bella's thighs. Beside them, Alex had refocused as soon as the Wolf had made his declaration, his jaw clenching as he watched the Wolf fondling Bella.

"On your knees, Toy," the Wolf said, giving Alex a penetrating look. Bella squirmed as two of the Wolf's fingers slid into her pussy, coaxing the wetness from her soft folds, stretching the entrance. His other hand was still playing with her breasts, pinching her nipples just firmly enough to make her squirm.

Slowly, Alex went down to his knees, not even sparing a backward glance as Ken and Lisa were led away. His attention was entirely on the Wolf and Bella. Sometimes she truly did feel more like she was the toy, not Alex, and like both of the men were fighting over her.

The Wolf's hand on her breast slid upward, to wrap around her throat, forcing her head backward so that her back arched and her breasts thrust forward. Her hands had fallen to her side, but Bella didn't move them, didn't try to keep the Wolf from touching her however he wished. The firm grip on her throat didn't hurt, and wasn't cutting off her air, but it did serve to emphasize her vulnerability. Made her feel even smaller and more helpless, because she knew that she didn't dare try to stop him. He could easily tighten his grip if she did.

"Give Toy some lube," the Wolf ordered one of the men, who immediately moved to do his bidding.

Bella couldn't see the Wolf's expression, but she swore she could feel his eyes glowing behind her.

"He's going to get Pet ready for me."

She whimpered, writhing as his fingers swirled in her pussy, his wet thumb coming up to smear her clit with her juices. The soldier handed Alex the lube, and he took it, his expression stony.

"Lift up your legs, Pet," the Wolf murmured into her ear. "Give Toy access to that pretty little asshole. You want him to be able to do a good job lubing you up for me, don't you?"

It was a humiliating position, leaning back against the Wolf and raising her knees in the air, keeping them spread far apart. She could feel his cock grinding against her ass, partially wedged between her cheeks as the tip of it pressed against her lower back. Her pussy and asshole were completely on display, so that anyone looking up at the dais would be able to see the Wolf's fingers as they frigged her pussy, keeping the folds splayed open.

Then Alex's fingers were pressing against her anus and Bella groaned as the tight hole gave way under pressure, opening for him. Both men had their fingers buried inside of her, moving and pressing against the walls of her body. As always, her asshole burned as it was penetrated, although the slight pain quickly receded to a more pleasant sensation, especially as the Wolf worked her pussy.

She could only imagine how she looked, with her legs wantonly spread and two men fingering her holes. Alex wasn't looking at her face anymore, his eyes were on the sight before him, entranced by the fingers moving back and forth inside of her. Her pussy lips were coated with her cream, so much that it was sliding down into her crack and helping to lubricate his fingers as they moved in and out of her ass.

———

The wet musky scent of feminine pleasure made him want to lean forward and lick, her clit standing out like a tempting little pink berry that the Wolf's thumb would occasionally flick, making her tighten down on both of them. Even though he hated that the Wolf was also touching her, that didn't stop his erection from straining as he pushed his fingers back and forth in her ass. Strangely he didn't give a shit that the Wolf might soon be doing something similar with Lisa. He was just glad that soon Bella would be free from this.

"Stop, Toy, I think she's ready," the Wolf said.

Alex hated that he listened. Reluctantly pulling his fingers from her body, he sat back. At this point, there was no way he was risking further punishment. Not when they were so close to being released. Somehow, he was going to find a way to stop what the Wolf was doing...

Even if he was made to forget, eventually he would remember, he promised himself.

The Wolf lifted Bella up, and Alex was forced to watch, his face only a foot away as the older man lined his cock up with Bella's ass. She moaned, whimpering as her tight hole was forced open, gravity pulling her down onto the Wolf's cock.

"Lick her pussy, Toy."

Holding her thighs open with his hands underneath them, the Wolf offered up Bella's pussy. Alex leaned forward, and slid his tongue up the center of her folds, making her gasp and rock on the Wolf's cock. Careful not to let his tongue get anywhere near the slick length that was sliding into her, Alex licked up and down her slit, knowing that her soft moans of pleasure were for him.

His cock throbbed as her sweet flavor coated his tongue, but he didn't touch it. It was one thing to get off because the Wolf was forcing him to, another to jerk himself while Bella's ass was being used by the crime lord. Moving up to her clit, he sucked on the swollen nub and she cried out, rocking her hips as she sank fully onto the Wolf's cock.

———

The sensations were intense. The angle of the Wolf's penetration made him feel huge in her ass, like he was stretching her wider than ever. It was a slow slide down his pole, impaling herself as gravity demanded, and then Alex's tongue started licking up her slit and she clenched, increasing the burn as her sphincter tried to tighten and couldn't. Even though the Wolf's hand was no longer on her throat, as he was holding her thighs wide open and supporting her, her head rested on his shoulder, her body arching and squirming as the pain and pleasure mixed together.

Alex sucked her clit into his mouth and her asshole spasmed, her hands coming down on his head and holding him tightly against her pussy as the Wolf filled her completely and her body exploded in orgasm from the combination. The suction on her clit increased and she rocked on the Wolf's cock, her asshole clenching and massaging the thick girth it was impaled on, as her pussy spasmed emptily.

When she finally fell back with a whimper, her fingers loosening their hold on Alex's hair, the Wolf's cock was still rock-hard in her backside and Alex was laving slow, tender licks up the center of her pussy. The swollen, sensitive folds tingled as she panted for breath.

"Stand up, Toy, and fuck Pet with me."

The Wolf leaned his chair back, his hands holding her wide open, as Alex slowly stood. His cock jutted out in front of him, achingly hard. Bella moaned, her eyes closing.

The head of Alex's cock pressed against her pussy and she quivered as he began to push in. The two cocks jostled for room inside of her body, stretching her, making her burn. Her pussy was already exquisitely sensitive from her orgasm, her anal muscles straining from the prolonged stretch of accommodating the Wolf's cock, and yet she still felt pleasure flare as Alex slowly worked his cock back and forth until he was completely buried inside of her, bending over both her and the Wolf.

Letting go of her thigh, the Wolf reached around her, grasping Alex by the throat, his thumb running over Alex's pulse.

"Fuck her. Hard."

———

Alex didn't want to obey, but his body did anyway. The tight, wet, silky heat of Bella's pussy was gripping him like a vise, and nature demanded that he move. When he did, he didn't have the control to go slowly. The Wolf's hand tightened on his throat as he thrust hard, rocking her on the Wolf's cock. He could feel the thick, hard ridge of the Wolf's dick rubbing against his as he fucked Bella, groaning with pleasure as she arched between them in growing ecstasy.

They all moved together, Alex braced over them, the Wolf surging up from underneath, and Bella caught in the middle, crying out with pleasure that was lightly tinged with flickering flames. The hand on Alex's throat was almost caressing him, impossible to ignore, even as he pounded into Bella, his balls tightening as his orgasm approached.

Then, just as the his sack tightened and his spine tingled, the Wolf suddenly pulled him down by the throat. Their mouths clashed together; the second Alex opened his lips in shock, the Wolf's tongue thrust in. Between them, Bella shuddered and screamed as ecstatic rapture shot through her, her holes spasming around their cocks, milking them.

The pleasure was so intense that Alex forgot to fight, forgot to try and pull away, and his mouth remained locked with the Wolf's as his muscles tightened and his cum spurted deep into Bella's pussy. He could feel the Wolf's cock throbbing alongside his, filling her ass with hot fluid, the three of them orgasming together, setting each other off, extending their shared pleasure.

When he was empty, Alex's knees felt so weak that he pulled out of Bella rather abruptly, sinking down between her and the Wolf's legs as his muscles went limp. It put him right on eye level with her pussy, which was glossy and dripping cum down onto the Wolf's balls. The other man's cock was slowly shrinking, Bella's reddened anus tightly gripping it even as it dwindled in size.

The scent of sex and cum was all that Alex could smell, burrowing into his brain. He wondered if even the Wolf's drugs could ever make him forget it.

19

As they were herded into the shuttle, Bella gripped Alex's hand. The dress that she'd been given to wear felt odd, the fabric rubbing against her skin. Even her undergarments were uncomfortable, despite the fact that they were made from the softest fibers available. And not just because her pussy and anus were still sore from when Alex and the Wolf had double-teamed her barely an hour before. She'd been without clothing for so long that it felt unnatural to be wearing any.

But that wasn't what was making her anxious.

"I don't understand," she whispered to Alex, unconsciously angling herself so that she was partially tucked against him, seeking comfort as she had so often done.

After the Wolf had finished with them, they'd both been taken from the room to shower. Then they'd been handed the clothing they were currently wearing, blindfolded, and taken out to a hover-car. At first Bella had panicked, thinking that the chips the Wolf had had put in them on their first day would react, but one of the soldiers had reassured her that it had been deactivated.

His words had proven true as they'd been driven away from the compound and nothing happened. Bella wondered if the Wolf had lied about the chips. Something had been injected into them that first day, but maybe not what they'd been told. Maybe it had been nothing more than one of the Wolf's mind games. The blindfolds had been removed as soon as they'd reached the shuttle port and they'd been escorted out of the car and onto the shuttle.

What hadn't happened was what both of them had been expecting—the memory drug.

Alex squeezed her hand reassuringly, although she could see the tension in his shoulders and jaw, suggesting that he was just as disturbed by the deviation. Was the Wolf planning on sending them back with their full memories? The shuttle had the Moon's logo on it, so the moment they set foot on it, they should be safe from him.

But how safe? Considering that the Moon's Prime, Second, Prime Commander and Earth Minister all had some kind of deal with the devil going on?

"No matter what happens," Alex whispered in her ear, his voice grave and determined, "I'll take care of you. I promise."

A bubbly blonde stewardess headed toward them from the back of the shuttle, beaming brightly. "Oh, look at you two! Please, come and sit down, everyone's going to be so excited when you arrive!"

Despite the sincerity of her friendliness and excitement, Bella couldn't help but eye the woman with suspicion. She was more confused now than she had ever been at the compound. Could they trust the stewardess?

The woman got them buckled in efficiently enough, babbling the entire time about how excited they must be to go home. Truthfully, Bella wasn't sure if she was excited. In fact, she felt a little sick to her stomach. What was going to happen when they got there? How could they prove that the top officials in the Moon's government had corrupt dealings with the Wolf?

Why did they still have their memories?

Being a captive inside the Wolf's compound had been far simpler than this.

Bella looked around the shuttle as the stewardess finished buckling them in, telling them that they'd be lifting off in just a few minutes, as another question rose in her brain.

Where was Trish?

————

"You have a choice." Jordan stood over her, his arms crossed over his chest, his eyes glinting as he looked down at her.

Shifting nervously, Trish folded her hands on her lap, trying not to squirm under that stern gaze. Something about the way he was looking at her made her feel even more nervous than usual. "I'm... retiring, for the lack of a better word. I have all the money I need and a place on an island near the equator. The Wolf is going to promote Zadia in my place and will only call on me if he has need."

Trish stared up at him silently, tensing as she wondered what this meant for her. For the first time, she saw Jordan hesitate, his hand coming up to rub along his jaw in an almost nervous gesture.

"You can come with me."

"Or... stay here?" she asked, her voice a whisper. That didn't appeal at all. She'd much rather go with him.

"Or go home."

"Home?" she echoed, as if she didn't know the meaning of the word. Truthfully, she just didn't quite understand what he was saying. It didn't compute.

"To the Moon." Jordan glanced at the timepiece on his wrist. "Alex and Bella will leave for the shuttle in ten minutes. You can go with them or stay here with me."

Her heart was beating so hard and fast that she was sure she could hear it in her ears. Go home? Escape this... sexual servitude? This man who had taken her against her will and used her as his personal sex toy?

Home to... what? People who looked down on her, a society that was rotten from the inside out, where wealth was valued over common sense and work ethic... home where no one had even cared that she was missing...

"What would I do, if I stayed?" she heard herself asking, her voice sounding far away, and like a stranger's.

Jordan stepped closer, his hand reaching out to cup her chin, fingers stroking her cheek softly. "The same thing we've been doing. Be mine. Decorate my home. Sleep in my bed. Let me take care of you."

It was that last one that sent a shiver down her spine. The gentle way he said it, the way his voice and eyes softened.

"Why me?" she asked, her voice husky. She sucked her lower lip in, wetting it, even though her mouth felt dry. It was the question she'd asked herself from the beginning.

There was a long silence, tension stretching between them, and she thought he might not answer. Then he sighed, his face carefully blank of all emotion, "Because I don't want to let you go."

From a man like Jordan, it was probably the most emotionally revealing statement she was going to get. It might as well be an avowal of love. Maybe it was just possession, but he was always gentle with her, always caring, always cherishing. A man didn't ask his possession if it wanted to stay with him. He didn't give his possession a choice.

Trish wavered for only a moment. Perhaps she had gone insane. Perhaps this was Stockholm Syndrome and she should be going home to throw herself at the mercy of a shrink. Instead, she nodded her head.

"I'll go with you."

Emotion flashed in Jordan's eyes, hot and triumphant, and he suddenly crouched down so that they were on eye level, his fingers firming on her jaw. Holding her immobile. Something warm and tingly pulsed through her core in response.

"Say it again, babygirl," he murmured. Demanded, really. His gaze bore into hers with a neediness that shocked her.

"I'll go with—"

Just as she started to say 'you,' he was on her, his mouth covering hers, lifting her up and moving her further back on the bed, covering her body with his. Hard muscle pinned her to the bed and she whimpered as hot need swirled. It might be sick, but she didn't care anymore. Here, she was wanted. Needed. Pleasured. Cared for. Cherished.

Her hands were pushed above her head as Jordan groaned with need, his tongue thrusting into her mouth even as his hips ground against her pussy. Holding her wrists in one hand, he used his other to yank her thighs up and open, and then undo the front of his pants. He was like a starving man, hungry for her, needing to lay and confirm his claim now that she'd made her decision.

Trish gasped as he thrust inside of her, hot and hard and completely impatient, filling her with his cock. She was wet enough that it didn't matter, even though her inner muscles strained to take him so quickly. Moaning, she gave in, submitting herself and sinking into the pleasure as he took her. It was so easy to just let go and be free.

And her ecstasy soared.

———

"Excuse me," Bella said, as the stewardess was about to turn away. "Where is Trish?"

"Who?" The stewardess looked at her, confused.

Alex frowned. Guilt slid through him as he realized he hadn't even thought about what had happened to Trish. He'd been so focused on Bella and relieved that she was getting to safety. Granted, everything he'd seen of the other young woman had shown that she was being treated differently—better in some ways—than he and Bella had been in the compound, like she'd been accepted there, but it grated on him that he'd let her fate slip his mind. It bothered him even more than the stewardess looked confused.

"The other woman who was taken at the same time as us? The blonde?" Bella persisted, looking even more concerned.

"Oh." Recognition dawned on the stewardess' face. "I think I remember something about her from the news vids. They really didn't say much though. I guess she doesn't have any family or something?" The stewardess shrugged, completely unconcerned. "No one told me, they just said that you two were going home. I'm sure she'll be sent home eventually; the Wolf never keeps anyone for more than a year. You two are much more important, your families never stopped funding the search for you. They said so on the news." She smiled brightly at them.

Rage boiled up inside Alex, and only Bella's sudden taking of his hand kept him from snapping at the stewardess. It was obvious that she didn't think Trish mattered at all. Or that there was anything really wrong with the ordeal they'd just gone through. It was an attitude typical of the Moon—as long as no one important was really affected, then it didn't matter.

Taking a deep breath, he closed his eyes and focused his thoughts on Bella.

Bella clothed. Bella beside him. Bella safe.

When they got to the Moon, he'd find a way to find out what happened to Trish and rescue her too.

Completely oblivious, the stewardess told them to have a good flight, and he heard her scuttle away. Bella's fingers stroked his, as though she was drawing comfort from him as well. Letting out a long breath, he felt the tension in his shoulders slowly dissipate. Releasing her hand, he wrapped his arm around her shoulders and she snuggled in as much as the seats would allow.

He wondered what would happen when they got to the Moon. Would they be met by the Prime? Prime Second or Commander? Ken's father? Threats to keep quiet about what had happened to them down there on Earth?

Alex smiled grimly. He might keep quiet for a while, as he planned, but there was no way he was going to let them get away with their corrupt dealings. The Moon needed to actually be independent of the Earth, so that they were no longer beholden to the crime lords for their necessities. They needed to stop allowing young men and women to be captured and abused as part of the exchange. On Earth, Alex had learned too much. Both about what was actually going on, and about himself. He was stronger than the weak-willed bastards who called themselves leaders.

There was no way they could keep him quiet. Not for long.

20

Bright light seemed to pierce right through her eyelids and she moaned. Her head hurt abominably. She reached up to tentatively touch her forehead, and moaned again. The skin felt tight. Tingly. Painful sparks seemed to radiate from where her fingertips had pressed so gently against her skin.

"I know, sweetheart. I know it hurts, just give us a moment."

A woman's soft voice, meant to be soothing, but it was like grating metal to her ears. She whimpered.

Something pressed against her neck and she recognized the hiss of a pressurized shot. Blessed cool relief slid through her and this time her moan was pure gratitude. Opening her eyes, she had to blink several times as her eyes adjusted to the light and the stark white of the ceiling and walls. She was lying on her back in what looked like a med-space.

A gentle-looking older woman with dark brown hair peered down, checking over her. "How are you feeling?"

"It doesn't hurt anymore." Her mouth felt strange, dry. "Water?"

"Of course, here you go."

"Thank you." She lifted the bottle to her mouth and nearly sighed with happiness as the water washed away the strange taste on her tongue. Looking around, she felt a small chill as she lowered the bottle. "Where am I? What happened?"

The woman peered at her again. "Do you remember your name?" she asked, instead of answering either of the questions.

Strangely, it didn't come to her immediately.

"Bella?" she said, but she heard her voice coming out more as though it was asking a question.

The woman smiled, pleased, and nodded her head. "What's the last thing you remember?"

That was harder. The answer didn't just pop into her head. She had to really think, and it kind of hurt, almost as if the answer was awakening the headache that she'd woken with.

"I was on Earth with Ken... and his friends Alex and Lisa..." And now she was in a med unit. Fear flashed through her. "Oh my god, were we in an accident? Where are they?"

"Shhh, shh, calm down," the woman urged, reaching out to take Bella's hands, rubbing her thumbs over the backs of them as she tried to sooth Bella. "There was no accident. You and Alex were kidnapped while you were on Earth, taken by the Wolf. You've just come home."

"Alex and I?" Bella murmured, confused, her brow winkling. But that didn't make sense. They'd gone down as a group of four for safety. Why would she and Alex have separated themselves from their significant others? Something swirled in her head, like a picture that wasn't quite coming together, but then the woman was talking again.

"We've found that being taken by the Wolf, especially for as long a period of time as you and Alex were, is incredibly traumatic," the woman explained, earnest and sincere. The warm kindness in her voice helped to calm Bella much more than her words did. "It's best to administer a drug which makes you forget your time down there, so that you can continue your normal life here. You don't have to worry about any aftereffects. We've been doing this for a while. The government pays for the treatment, at no cost to the Wolf's victims." Her eyes flashed a bit angrily. "One day that monster is going to get what he deserves."

"I... see..." Bella said. Except that she didn't, not entirely. What the woman said made sense, and she was obviously sincere in her emotions, but Bella had the strangest feeling that everything she was saying was wrong.

With a sympathetic look on her face, the woman released Bella's hands, patting them. "I know, it's an adjustment. You've been gone for several months, but it feels like nothing, right? Don't worry, it won't take you too long to adjust. We're releasing you from the hospital today and you'll be able to slide right back into your old life."

"Okay..." Bella rubbed her head. It felt like there was something inside her brain, trying to get out. "Can I see Alex?" For some reason it felt imperative that she find Alex as soon as possible. She wasn't sure why. Maybe just because the woman had told her that they'd been through their ordeal together. They weren't exactly close, although she'd always admired him.

The pressure on her brain seemed to tighten, the more she thought about him.

"Yes, of course," the woman answered, looking somewhat relieved. "Come on, let's get you dressed and I'll take you to him."

It only took a few minutes for Bella to put on her clothes. They felt strange, unnatural, although she didn't know why. Maybe she was still disoriented. It was very odd to know that she'd been on Earth for months and yet she couldn't remember any of it. She recalled seeing the victims of the Wolf being released from the hospital, the blank looks on their faces. This must be why they never answered the media's questions; because they couldn't remember.

Maybe the woman was right and it was a blessing. She shouldn't want to remember.

Right?

They entered a room that looked more like a lobby. Alex was sitting there on a couch, leaning forward and resting his arms on his elbows, speaking to a man seated in front of him. As Bella and the woman came in, Alex looked up and something in his expression cleared, relief showing stark across his face.

"Bella!"

He jumped up and she found herself lurching forward, practically throwing herself into his arms. Her body had moved before she had time to think about it, but once she was pressed against him, his arms tight around her, she immediately relaxed. It felt familiar. Safe. If they'd been captured together then they must have leaned on each other, so that only made sense.

The man and woman had moved together and were talking in low voices, seeming surprised about Alex and Bella's reactions to each other.

"Are you okay?" Alex murmured, keeping his voice low as he pulled away to look down at her.

Even under their current circumstances, she couldn't help but notice how attractive he was. How drawn to him she was. Shouldn't she be feeling guilty about that? After all, Ken was her boyfriend... but surprisingly she didn't feel guilty at all. And when she thought about Ken, all she got was a kind of sick, unhappy feeling. But why?

"I'm okay... just confused. They said we were taken by the Wolf, but I can't remember anything," she whispered, letting some of her consternation show.

"I know... the last thing I remember is being really angry, but I can't remember why." His brow furrowed as he pulled her closer.

Bella liked the way it felt.

"Angry? When we were on Earth?"

"Yeah... I think it had something to do with Lisa, but I just can't remember what." His frustration was clear in his voice, but his words were doing something to her. Stirring some kind of emotional response that seemed to be attached to a memory.

"I think... I remember being mad too... at Ken..." she said slowly, trying to sort through her feelings and the memories that seemed to be little more than wisps floating through her head. "Mad and sad."

"I don't know what happened to us, but I'm going to take care of you, Bella, okay?" Alex pulled her in again, tucking her head beneath his chin and she nestled in like it was the most natural thing in the world. It felt right.

"Okay."

"Get your hands off her!" The door slammed open and Bella jumped, instinctively clutching at Alex as he practically shoved her behind him, already moving into a defensive stance, ready to protect her from whatever was after them.

The man and woman in the room with them both jumped as Ken's father came barreling in. Bella had always been intimidated by him, but she'd grown to like him too. Now, looking at him, something in the pit of her stomach roiled and she felt like throwing up. Her instincts jibbered and shrieked, telling her to flee. Since she couldn't, she just clutched at Alex's back, holding him in place, while simultaneously clinging to him for comfort.

"What the hell?" Alex asked harshly, one hand in front of him to help fend off Ken's father, the other behind him as if to herd Bella. "What are you doing here?"

"Keep my son's girlfriend safe, apparently," Ken's father said, glaring and stabbing an accusing finger at Alex. "He's been kidnapped, taken by the Wolf, just days ago and you're already trying to steal her away from him?"

The way that Ken Sr. was looking at her made Bella's skin crawl. She shuddered, not knowing why. It was an unusual reaction. He looked angry, which wasn't a surprise considering that Ken had apparently been recently taken, but...

Why didn't she feel upset about that? If anything, she felt a strange sense of... what? Vindication? Justice?

An image formed in her mind of Ken... begging. Naked. With a woman, also naked, by his side, also begging... Alex. Ken and Lisa, begging her and Alex not to be upset. Bella moaned as she pressed her fingers to her temples as the images became clearer, her emotions rioting and bringing them back. Strong emotions.

Anger. Betrayal. Hurt. Pain. Loss.

She shook her head to clear her mind, only now noticing that Alex was holding her again, his voice filled with worry as he said her name.

"I'm okay," she said, shakily.

Ken Sr. stepped forward and she cringed back as Alex snarled at him. The man that Alex had been talking with reached out and pulled Ken Sr. back.

"But I'm not Ken's girlfriend. He cheated on me with Lisa. We broke up. That's how we—Alex and I—got captured. We left them in the hotel where they'd been... Anyway, we left, and they took us from taxi."

Tension filled Alex's arms. "That's right," he said, his voice going hard. "I remember now."

———

If Alex hadn't been looking directly at Ken Sr., he would have missed the consternation and something that looked a lot like fear flitting across his face. Bella nuzzled into Alex's chest, and he tightened his arms around her. Since he'd woken up he'd been confused, agitated, and a bit angry. Now, with Bella in his arms, some of that was soothed.

Whatever had happened down on Earth, he instinctively knew that no matter what, he had to take care of Bella. It wasn't logical, he didn't know—or at least didn't remember why—but that was what he felt.

It was like a sensory memory, something that he just instinctively knew.

Ken Sr. turned to the doctor, the man that Alex had been talking to. He could only assume the woman who had come in the room with Bella was another doctor. Their furious, whispered conversation wasn't entirely audible to him, but he realized that he was picking up much more of it than he would have thought possible. Almost as if he was used to listening in to conversations like this.

"...how can they be remembering? That shouldn't be..."

"... close to the initial event that we aimed for.... no other explanation.... shouldn't remember any more...."

"Give them more of the drug."

".... too dangerous. They've already had the maximum.... possible he did something..."

Bella murmured something against Alex's chest. Distracted, he looked down at her, stroking her brown hair as he held her tenderly. He remembered Lisa cheating on him. His rage at the betrayal, both by her and his best friend. Practically dragging Bella out of the hotel, convincing her that she deserved better than a cheating ass like Ken.

Something else though, too. Holding her protectively... while they were naked, on a bed. Feeling... tenderness... protectiveness... love... joy. All very strongly. The emotions seemed to be key. They came first, followed by images. Impressions. Memories that slowly became clearer, stronger.

"Come on, Bella, I'll take you to your family." Ken Sr. had stepped away from the doctors again.

Alex didn't like the glint in his eye. Something else stirred in the back of his mind, farther away, attached to anger. Maybe it was just residual, leftover from his anger over Ken Jr.

"No!" Bella's voice came out panicked as she turned slightly, holding onto Alex even tighter. "I want to stay with Alex."

"Sir, it's best if you not distress them," the male doctor said.

Alex realized that the man had never given Alex his name.

"We'll take them to their families."

Bella made a small noise of distress and the doctor looked over, giving her a reassuring smile.

"Both of you together, of course."

Ken Sr. looked as if he wanted to countermand the doctor's orders, but the woman gave him a sharp look and he subsided, allowing them to be led away. Something close to hatred stirred in Alex's chest, and he felt like he could almost remember why... and then they were leaving the room and it faded just as quickly as it had come.

21

"I'm doing okay, mom, I promise," Bella said.

It had been two weeks since she and Alex had returned home to the Moon, their memories wiped. Two weeks of trying to get them back. Maybe they should just leave it alone, but they couldn't seem to stop poking at them.

Especially because sometimes, something came through.

Bella had had a particularly bad spot on her second day home when her parents had wanted to take her to the doctor. She'd had a full-blown hysterical panic attack, that only calmed when Alex held her, reassuring her that she didn't have to go. Her parents, terrified of her response, had quickly agreed. That hadn't stopped the memories from cascading back. Not all of them, of that she was sure, but she remembered Doctor Margolis. Remembered his cruel smile, the electricity that he'd tortured her with...

When her parents had left, she'd told Alex about it. His resulting fury had made him remember a name—

Nurse Roche. Although he couldn't remember why he knew that name. It just popped into his head.

Eventually they figured out that the more strongly they'd felt about something, the more likely it was they'd be able to remember it eventually. Sometimes it burst out, like an explosion in their minds, other times it came more gradually. Alex was constantly protective of Bella. The other day they'd been nearly caught out by media, who had realized their location when they'd gone to get groceries, and a young, blonde-haired woman had almost been injured when she'd been knocked over. Alex had gone practically ballistic, yelling at the media, protecting both Bella and the young woman with his body until security showed up.

When they got home, he told her about Trish. He remembered her more clearly than Bella did. They'd started trying to look up what might have happened to her, but there was no real news coverage of her kidnapping, nothing to indicate where she might be now. There was plenty about Bella and Alex though, including clips from Ken and Lisa begging for their return. It had sent Alex into another ranting rage that Bella had calmed by cuddling with him.

They hadn't had sex. Not yet. Alex was being a gentleman and Bella... well, Bella was getting impatient. She was living in his house, sleeping in his bed, in his arms, every night, and yet the few times she'd tried to initiate, he'd been too worried that they were reacting to things they couldn't remember. Too worried that she was emotionally vulnerable and that he would be taking advantage of her.

At this point, Bella was starting to think she was going to need to take advantage of him.

At the moment, she was alone. Alex had gone out to look for a job. The government was funding them right now, kind of a grant for the trauma they'd been through—even though they couldn't remember it—but Alex felt a pressing need to do something. Maybe something political, he'd said. Bella hadn't entirely understood, and she didn't like being separated from him during the day, but she was learning to deal. And it did give her more time to try and remember things.

They'd quickly learned that it was frowned upon though. They'd been in touch with a few of the Wolf's former victims, none of whom wanted to even try and remember what had happened to them. They'd looked askance when Alex and Bella had even hinted that some things were coming back to them. The next day, a doctor had dropped by, nearly sending Bella into another panic attack. She hadn't been at all like the doctors that had taken care of Bella and Alex when they'd first woken up. She'd been stern, uncompromising, and had told them that they could damage their own brains by trying to force memories to return. They needed to concentrate on reestablishing their lives, not on the past.

Of course that was kind of hard to do when so many things about her life made Bella unhappy. She couldn't stand to be around Ken's father, although his parents had both tried to reach out to her and Alex. Living at home wasn't an option; she had too many panic attacks at night when she wasn't with Alex. Her cheating boyfriend had disappeared, presumed a captive of the Wolf. Ken's parents were funding the search for him and his and Lisa's faces were on the media almost every day. Interest had soared, since they had already been known from Alex and Bella's ordeal.

"You aren't going to watch the broadcast, are you? I don't want you to be all alone when you see it. At least wait for Alex if you won't watch it with us," her mother pleaded through the line.

"Of course, mom, I'll wait for Alex," Bella said, lying through her teeth.

Today, for the first time ever, the Wolf was going to be broadcasting a message to the Earth's media. It was also going to be playing on the Moon. If Alex wasn't back in time, Bella would be watching it alone, because there was no way she could wait. She needed to see the man who had held her captive for months. To see if it would spark something—anything—in her memory. Sometimes it felt like her memories were right there, on the other side of a wall, pounding at it and trying to get through.

Finally she managed to convince her mother that she was just fine and get off of the phone with her. She knew her parents meant well, but sometimes they drove her up the wall. It was like they expected her to be broken, and that's how they treated her. But she wasn't. Even with the things she remembered, she didn't feel broken. Sometimes, even when she remembered something awful, like her time with Dr. Margolis, she felt stronger afterward. Because she'd come through it.

Half an hour later, after a lot of channel-flipping, the broadcast finally started. Alex still wasn't home. Curling up with a cushion between her thighs and her chest, Bella turned the channel to the news.

The first thing that struck her was the man himself. The media had tried for so long to get a good, clear picture of him and had never achieved it. But the moment she saw him, there on the screen, she felt something inside of her shift in confirmation.

Yes, that's what he looks like.

It was him. Not an actor or an impostor, like some of the reporters had theorized would show up. That was the man himself. Bright-green piercing eyes, a hard face, and dark- black hair that was silver around his temples.

One of the reporters said something mocking about that sign of age that had been allowed. Idiot. As if a bit of grey hair somehow made the Wolf less powerful. He had no need to cling to his youth to create an imposing presence, he was imposing all on his own.

The image began to zoom out and Bella tensed. Something inside of her recognized the location. A dais, with the Wolf in the center, seated in a chair that was almost a throne. On either side of him, kneeling and naked—although their genitals had been blurred out by the censors—were Lisa and Ken. Behind him hung two black-bordered banners with a sigil on them.

There was a roaring noise in her ears, drowning out whatever the reporters were saying as she stared at the sigil. It looked like an S with a horizontal bar through the top curve. Nothing that should have meant anything. Definitely nothing that should have sent a strong surge of emotion through her.

It was one of the few strong, positive emotional reactions that she'd had. The only one she'd had that didn't have to do with Alex. Bella licked her lips, trying to distance herself and study what she was feeling. Excitement. Joy. Hope. But why? Why would that sigil elicit those feelings?

The pressure seemed to be building in her head, and then all of a sudden the camera zoomed in on the Wolf again and Bella nearly cursed. Her focus was lost and the pounding receded. It wasn't the first time that had happened when she was trying to remember something and it wouldn't be the last. She made herself attend to what the Wolf was saying, hoping it would bring something back.

Nothing. He was addressing the people of Earth, declaring how important he was. Telling them that he had the son of a government official of the Moon at his beck and call. When prompted, Ken stood and spread his legs apart, bending forward. A woman came up, very pretty with red hair, and began to spank Ken with her hand as the Wolf continued to talk.

The cameraman was apparently too fascinated by what was happening to Ken to zoom back in on the Wolf, although he didn't zoom in in Ken either. Probably worried for his job if he did something so blatant. This was the first time the media was getting a look at the Wolf's sexual decadence.

Something about it all rang completely wrong to Bella. She noticed that the Wolf kept gesturing up to the sigil, which drew her eye again, as he began to talk about how all those loyal to him should wear it. Declare themselves for him. Because the Moon was using too many of the Earth's resources, stealing them from those who labored for them, and it was time to put an end to it. His words seemed to filter in and out of her ears, meaningless babble as she felt the hope and joy growing in her chest the longer she stared at that sigil.

Her hand reached out as if to touch it...

And she jerked back as the door opened.

<h1 style="text-align:center">22</h1>

The guilty look on Bella's face as Alex came in the door told him all he needed to know. She was watching the broadcast, even though she'd said she would wait for him. He sighed, but he wasn't truly angry. Somehow he'd known. But there was something else in her expression too, the kind of excitement that she usually showed just before she remembered something new.

"Come here," she said, the guilt washing away quickly as she pointed at the screen. "Look at that, on the banner behind him... do you feel anything?"

Anger, as he looked at the Wolf, but nothing specific enough to spark a single memory. Probably there were too many tied up with the man. But he did recognize him, immediately, and knew that he was the real deal. Alex barely glanced at Ken and Lisa, although his attention lingered on the redhead for a moment. Looking at her made his balls ache, and not in the good way that he associated with being around Bella.

Then he looked at the banners that Bella was so excited about. His chest tightened, and it took him a moment before he realized he felt rising excitement too. Excitement and... triumph?

The dark hole in the back of his mind opened up, except that it wasn't dark, there was light in it, like a tunnel...

"A tunnel, yes," Bella said, her head jerking back around to stare at the television. The same hope and excitement that he felt in his chest was glowing on her face.

He hadn't even realized he'd spoken out loud. Her hand reached out as if to touch the sigil.

"The way out... Alex, we knew the way out!"

Fuck.

He groaned as he went to his knees, gripping his head in his hands. It wasn't just that one memory that had become unblocked, it was like they were all coming tumbling through the tunnel, one after other, assaulting him from every side.

"Alex? Alex are you okay?"

The panic in Bella's voice made him want to leap up and take down whatever was scaring her, but how could he protect her from himself? He hadn't been able to at the Wolf's compound. Hadn't been able to when they'd been returned the Moon, forcibly separated after landing, and then given the memory drugs. Not that the doctors had realized what they were blocking the memories for. Alex was pretty sure that they truly believed they were help-ing, that Alex and Bella had been traumatized by their time with the Wolf and needed protection.

Those fucking Moon officials...

"Bella... I remember everything." His voice cracked. With his eyes closed, so that he couldn't look at her face, all he could see was the memories rushing by, filling that empty, gaping hole. "The things I did to you..."

"Alex, you wouldn't, you always took care of me, I know that," Bella said, rubbing her hand over his shoulders trying to soothe him. "I don't remember everything, but I *know* that."

The faith in her voice, the trust, made him feel like he was splintering apart inside. He could remember how much he'd enjoyed fucking her. Dominating her. The sick part of him that had become aroused whenever the Wolf had fucked her too. Down there it hadn't seemed quite as bad; now, having been back, no longer in the situation, all he could do was pick apart every single thing he'd done.

He was a monster, and she didn't even see it.

Growling, he grabbed her wrist, pulling her down onto the ground as she shrieked, and rolling atop her, pressing her lower body into the ground with his as she stared up at him. Despite that, once the surprise receded, she didn't look scared.

"I hurt you, Bella," he said, rocking against her, feeling his cock starting to grow as it rubbed against her softness. "I hurt you because he told me to."

"You protected me," she countered, shocking him as she wrapped her legs around him, arching beneath him. There was no way he could misinterpret the hot arousal filling her eyes as she tilted her chin challengingly. "I chose you. I remember choosing you, Alex. I remember you trying to fight him."

"Dammit, Bella, I'm a monster!" he yelled, trying to pull away from her.

She kept her legs wrapped tightly around him. Making a frustrated noise under her breath, Bella reached up and grabbed his head, pulling him down as her lips came up to meet his.

Idiot man. Then again, she wasn't entirely surprised at Alex's attempt to take the entire burden of guilt onto himself. Her memories were coming back. Not as quickly as Alex's had—that had looked painful as hell—but they were sliding back in one at a time. Most of them to do with Alex, many of them surrounded around her admiration for him, her appreciation of him, her love for him.

She remembered him hurting her. She also remembered him holding her as he told her why. She remembered them fucking, and she also remembered them making love. Alex's arms around her at night, creating a safe haven in the midst of uncertainty. Her fear for him as he tried to fight to keep her safe. The way he'd constantly put his own body between her and perceived danger.

Bella kissed him. Hard. Passionately.

Maybe the idiot didn't remember everything, maybe he was only remembering the bad, because right now she was remembering a lot of the good. His mouth tasted of mint and chocolate, his cock rocked against her pussy and she flooded with anticipation. Memories slid through her, both good and bad, many of them arousing her even though it made her feel a little ashamed to be turned on by them... but then again, she'd been turned on when they'd been happening to her.

"Bella..." Alex sounded tortured as he pulled his mouth away from hers, although he was no longer trying to detangle their bodies completely.

"Shut up," she said fiercely, glaring up at him. "I remember choosing you, Alex. I remember how guilty you felt when I did it, but I didn't feel any guilt until the Wolf took you instead. I always liked you, even when Ken and I were together. And while we were down there... I think... I know... I couldn't have made it through without you. You were everything to me. You still are."

His gaze softened, his fingers brushing over her cheek as she blinked back tears.

"I remember us touching. You holding me. I remember how much I liked it," she murmured, rubbing her hand over his chest, now that he seemed to be softening. Listening to her. The intense look in his eyes didn't go away though, it just shifted, changed... heated. "I think... I might have fallen in love with you down there, Alex."

Something flashed through his eyes. Hot. Possessive. Relieved. This time his lips came down on hers by choice, demanding and hard. Bella moaned into his kiss, thankful that he'd finally stopped being so gentle with her.

She tore at his shirt, and suddenly they were both in a frenzy to get each other's clothes off. To be skin to skin, the way they'd been so accustomed to. Neither of them even noticed the Wolf's voice droning on in the background—or if they did, it was subconsciously and it didn't distract either of them. With their memories fully returned, they were used to his presence.

Alex squeezed her breasts, his mouth coming down on one nipple and she writhed as his teeth scraped against the little bud.

"Harder," she pleaded, arching and thrusting her breasts up into his face, her fingers weaving through the dark locks of his hair. "Please, Alex."

He sucked harder, biting down as his fingers pinched her other nipple tightly and Bella shuddered as the sensation went straight to her pussy. She rocked, trying to rub herself against him, and was only able to reach his stomach. The hard length of his erection was pressing against her thigh, but not anywhere near enough to her pussy to satisfy her.

The rough manipulation of her sensitive nipples was making her wild, and she begged and pleaded for him as he toyed with her. It was hedonistic. Painful pleasure. All the things she'd reluctantly liked about their time with the Wolf, except without the humiliation, without the fear, without the shame. And it was with Alex. Just Alex.

When he moved up her body, taking her lips as his cock thrust into her pussy, Bella nearly orgasmed as their bodies aligned. She clung to him, moaning wildly as he began to slowly move back and forth, his large cock spearing her open and stretching her. After a steady diet of sexual contact with the Wolf, and then nothing for the past few weeks, she felt needier than ever... but she was also tight and needed the time to adjust to his size again.

One hand slid down her back and under her buttocks. Her juices were trickling down the crease of her bottom, and she felt his finger slide through them, rubbing over her anus. She tightened around him, her body stiffening as his finger rimmed the little hole, pressing gently on it. Part of her wanted to tell him no, while the rest of her screamed yes.

The sensitive bundle of nerves seemed to spark as the tip of his finger slid in, pumping gently as he continued to rise and fall over her, his tongue invading her mouth, so that it was like he was taking her in all three holes at once. Bella felt herself giving over to the sensations, giving in... submitting to Alex's protective dominance.

Ecstasy swirled through her, and she began to buck and writhe beneath him, her orgasm swelling higher.

It was sick, so sick, but he liked the stiffness of Bella's body as his finger first pierced her anus. He loved the surge of power that came when she didn't protest, when her slick pussy tightened around him and she gave herself over to pleasure instead, accepting him, all of him. The Wolf had shown him that there were some ways in which they were similar, but if she'd told him no, he would have honored that barrier.

That was how they were different.

And Alex clung to that.

But he couldn't deny the effect it had on him when she didn't tell him no.

His finger went deeper into that hot, tight channel, his thrusts becoming harder as she arched beneath him, crying out. The tremors of her pussy became spasms as her inner muscles clenched, trying to milk his cock. Alex groaned, crying out her name as his balls tightened and he swelled inside of her clasping heat. Fulling impaling her on both his cock and his finger, he groaned as he felt the pulses of his own dick against the digit in her ass, filling her pussy with cum.

Head bowed, he pulled his finger out, his cock jerking slightly at her soft whimper.

Still half-hard, still pressed inside of her, he kissed her lips, her nose, her eyes, enjoying the way she squirmed beneath him, her fingers stroking her skin. It was like rediscovering her now that their memories were back.

A long while later, still entangled on the floor, although now he was on his back and she was on her side, curled up against him with her head resting on his shoulder, they listened to the news anchors debating whether or not the Wolf meant to go to war with the Moon. They scoffed at the very idea, jeering his claim that the Moon couldn't last very long without the support of the earth. One of them laughed and said, "Didn't anyone tell him we're self-sufficient?"

But Bella and Alex knew differently. They remembered.

"What are we going to do?" she asked, softly, her fingers sliding through the hair on his chest, almost petting him. Alex found her gentle touch soothing, if a bit ticklish.

He'd been thinking the exact same thing. "We're going to tell them. Tell everyone. Okay?"

There was only the barest moment of hesitation before she nodded her head. "Okay."

23

Five Months Later

"Sir?" A man came running up to his desk, his face slightly panicked. "The report you wanted, Sir."

It only took a moment to scan and then he was shoving it back across the desk. "Get them out."

"Sir?"

"Send her a message. 'It's time to escape the cage and fly free,' along with the shuttle number and the meet time. We'll get them out tomorrow, with anyone who will come with them."

A small hand tugged on his pants from underneath his desk. "Master?"

Raising his eyebrow, he scooted back slightly so that he could look at the woman curled up there. She rarely tried to get his attention when he was busy, so he assumed that whatever she wanted, it must be important.

Dark eyes peered up at him, filled with worry. "Master, may I send a message to my parents?"

"Of course," he said, sliding his chair all the way back

so that she could scramble out. "And when you return, you will thank me properly for allowing you to do so."

"But of course, Master," she said cheekily, her curvy bottom jiggling as she turned to go with the soldier.

A thin smile curved his lips. She was not who he would have chosen to keep, but she had begged to stay and he was content enough. There was an old Earth saying—"If you love something, let it go. If it comes back, it's yours."

They weren't his, but he would still do what he could. In the meantime, his sweet Slut was devoted and she had begged, kicked and screamed to stay with him when he'd sent Bitch home a month ago. So he'd let her.

He hit the button on his desk that brought up his private vidphone. It only took a minute of chiming before the call was answered. The hard face that showed up was actually softer than it used to be, although just as familiar.

"We're sending a rescue mission tomorrow. Tell your girl to send her messages."

The other man's face relaxed even further. "Thank you, Sir. Do you want me to go up with them?

"Zadia will be going, but if you want to go, I'm not sure if it will help or hinder to see a familiar face."

"It might help, if I bring Trish," Jordan said, almost cheerfully. His eyes glinted; he was clearly looking forward to seeing some action again. "They've been trying to find out what happened to her, and she'll be able to reassure them."

Ah yes. Along with putting their lives in danger by telling anyone, and everyone, who would listen about the Moon government's duplicity, starting civil panic when people realized it was the truth, and attempting to overthrow the Moon's government with the more level-headed of its citizens, his former Toy and Pet had also sent video pleas to Earth asking for information about Trish. She'd been delighted and touched to know that someone cared. Unfortunately, when she'd tried to send a message back, they'd found communications had been blocked by the Moon's government.

The Moon was tearing itself apart. The only good news was that their issues hadn't touched Earth yet. Scott still had a few soldiers up there who kept him informed on the status. For a while it had looked as though Alex and his followers were going to be able to overthrow the government and make some changes, but there were too many who hadn't believed his and Bella's assertions, too many who hadn't wanted to believe, and the report he'd just received had said that the entire place was descending into violent anarchy.

Scott didn't particularly care, other than to get his people out. Alex and Bella too, if they would listen. If not, then they'd be forcibly removed from the situation.

Taking their choice away didn't particularly bother him either, although his brain knew it should. He understood ethics, and even allowed himself to be governed by some of them. To a point.

Slut came trotting back into the room, looking pleased. The message she'd recorded would be transmitted on private channels to the men he still had on the Moon, who would pass it along to her parents. Hopefully they'd listen and get the fuck out tomorrow. Although, from what his sweet slut had said, she wasn't particularly fond of them. They hadn't been very good to her, and the first time she'd been able to make choices for herself had actually been here on Earth. Where no one expected her to trade her body for power, to work her way up a ladder of men to the top of the heap. No, here all she had to do was please him and she was taken care of.

It turned out the position suited her admirably, especially with her penchant for pain.

"Thank you, Master," she said, looking up at him with adoring eyes as she knelt down, her hands already going to the front of his pants.

He leaned back, watching as she bent over his cock, taking it between her lips and swirling her tongue around the head in the way she knew he liked best. Groaning, he ran his hand through her hair, massaging her scalp as her mouth slid eagerly down the entire length of his shaft. Bobbing her head, she caressed his balls, her other hand sliding down so she could finger his anus as she sucked him deep.

"Good Slut... you want my cum don't you?" he murmured, half closing his eyes as he pretended her brown hair was slightly lighter and curly.

Her happy humming response vibrated along his dick, her tongue licking eagerly and he thrust upward and into her mouth, easily invading her throat.

When he came, he pressed her head to his groin, forcing himself completely inside of her mouth so that her nose was pressed against his belly. Hot cum jetted down her throat, which convulsed and massaged his cock as it spurted the creamy liquid straight into her stomach. Her finger in his ass massaged his prostate, milking him of every last drop as the intense orgasm shuddered through him.

With a low groan, he pulled her off of his cock, knowing from experience that she would keep sucking him until he was hard again if he let her. When he'd named her Slut, he hadn't known how prophetic he'd been.

Lips swollen, pupils dilated, she looked up at him, panting for breath and eager for more male attention.

"I have to get work done now," he told her, tightening his grip on her hair and enjoying the way her eyes unfocused in arousal. She was so easy. So eager. "Would you like to go back under my desk or would you like to go visit the doctor?"

A shudder went through her. "The doctor, please, Master," she said, as he knew she would.

Being given choices made her happy and it amused him. Sometimes she even surprised him with what she chose. Not today though. She loved it when he allowed her to visit Dr. Margolis, who had strict instructions not to do any permanent damage to her. He himself had no taste for the high levels of pain she sometimes craved, but he kept her visits to the doctor sparse. It was never good to overindulge.

He didn't bother watching her hurry out of the room, his mind already returning to work and to the pair on the Moon. There were plans to be made.

24

Alex couldn't believe his eyes. Not only was Trish standing in front of him, Jordan's hands on her shoulders and her eyes bright with happiness, but she wanted them to return to Earth?

He turned to his first in command, his right-hand man from the past months, someone he'd grown to trust almost as much as Bella. Ned looked back at him, his expression blank.

"You work for him, don't you?" Alex asked, his voice hard as he tried to contain his fury at the betrayal. "You work for the Wolf?"

"I pass messages," Ned replied, completely unrepentant as Bella gasped. "That's it. Nothing detrimental to you. He just wanted to know what was going on up here. With good reason." The other man glanced over Alex's shoulder, his eyes taking in the destruction of the Moon's hive-like housing system, the fires that were still burning and choking the air in the dome. "It's time for us to leave. There's nothing here to salvage."

"Alex—" Bella tugged on his sleeve, turning him partially toward her. "He might be right."

He groaned. "Not you, too. We swore we were going to see this out, remember?"

"And we have," she said, taking his face in her hands, cradling it. Comforting him, because she knew how much this would hurt him, to feel that he had failed in his mission. "They didn't want to change. You can't force people to accept that they have to change their way of life if they don't want to. We should take this, save those who want to change and are willing to work for it."

"Earth's already overpopulated." He shook his head, knowing that at least part of his resistance was because he didn't want to be in any way beholden to the Wolf. "We need this colony."

"No," Jordan said, at the same time that Trish started shaking her head. Her smile brightening even further as he spoke. "We need colonies. Ones that can actually be self-sufficient. Cora and Trace have been working on a space-craft that would actually be able to travel to other habitable planets. It will be ready within the next couple months." His cold blue eyes met Alex's. "The colony will need a leader."

Shock went through Alex as he stared at Jordan.

"Cora and Trace?" Bella squeaked, obviously just as shocked. "And it will have enough fuel? Food? How long have they been working on this?"

"Years. All of Earth has." Jordan snorted. "Did you think we on Earth were all truly content to do nothing but provide the Moon with our resources? To be treated as cogs in a machine, with nothing better to do than support people who barely looked at us as being human? We've been making ready our escape as well."

"What about Cora? And the Wolf?" Alex asked sharply, finding his voice. "They don't want to leave Earth?"

"No, why would they?" Jordan asked, raising his eyebrow. "They have their own empires already carved out. Life on the colonies is going to be hard. Probably low-tech. Besides, Trace and Cora need to stay on Earth to keep working on more projects. That woman's an engineering genius you know."

"A sadistic, self-centered sociopath, but a genius," Ned added. His light-green eyes looked imploringly at Alex. "Please, Sir. Save what you can. Start over. Let the Moon live out its own fate."

"Alex... I think they're right." Bella hugged her arms around him.

Trish was nodding. Jordan and Ned just stood there, waiting.

Closing his eyes, Alex took a deep breath. He could practically feel his parents, Bella's parents, his men and women that had tried so hard... many of them former victims of the Wolf whose memories had been restored. It hadn't taken long for the scientists on their side to realize that Alex and Bella had been pumped full of chemicals to counteract the memory drug that the Moon had administered. They'd told him that the doses had probably been administered over a course of weeks. Once they'd started examining former victims, they'd found traces of the same chemicals, prototypes to what Alex and Bella had received.

He didn't condone the Wolf's methods. He didn't understand how the man could be so callous, so sexually depraved even while he was trying to show the Moon captives what was actually going on, but he knew that there was only one real option for them. If they stayed, they'd eventually be killed by those who insisted that he was the real trouble. Who blamed him for all the unrest that had swept through the Dome.

That or they'd be killed when the Dome itself was destroyed. It was already well on its way.

"Alright. Fine."

———

Their time on Earth was almost anticlimactic. Alex had already known Lisa had stayed with the Wolf when Ken returned home. When he tried to convince her to come on the spaceship with him, she'd actually laughed at him. Told him he was a good man. Too good. Turned out she'd only gone out with him because her parents had told her to, they'd wanted her to use him to get to Ken. Which was exactly what she'd done before it had all fallen apart.

He still could barely comprehend that her parents would be so desperate for even more influence on the Moon's government than they'd already had. They hadn't accompanied Alex and the others down to Earth and Lisa didn't seem particularly put out about it.

Trish, too, had chosen to stay on Earth, with Jordan. She told Bella that she still was embarrassed by Jordan's exhibitionism, but she'd learned to enjoy it too. And she loved the way he took care of her. Bella thought Trish needed a good therapist, but who was she to talk?

Maybe a part of her understood a bit better when, the night before they were scheduled to leave, she walked into the apartment that she and Alex shared, and the Wolf was standing there. Staring out the window.

He turned, that piercing green gaze seeming to stab right through her. "Pet."

It sounded like an endearment and made her instantly, horrifyingly aroused.

"Bella," she corrected, in a faint but insistent voice. "What are you doing here?"

He studied her for a moment, his eyes slightly hooded. She clenched her hands into fists.

"Saying goodbye."

"I hope you don't plan to pull the same trick on Alex," she said, her mouth dry. "He'll kill you."

A confident, amused smile flashed across his face. "He could try. But no, I wasn't planning to. I didn't think he'd allow it."

But he would have liked to. That much was obvious. There wasn't a vast amount of emotion in his voice, but Bella hadn't realized how well she'd gotten to know his tones. His inflections. He sounded... almost wistful.

"Why?" she whispered. "Why did you do it?"

He shrugged. "At first? It was amusing. All those idiots coming down here, flaunting their wealth, acting as if they owned us, when truly, we owned them. A way to show at least a few that they weren't any better than us. Especially when I involved the Prime." He laughed. "Not that the Prime had a leg to stand on anyway. When we realized that they were making you all forget, that no one was going back and talking about anything that we'd told them... that's when we started to plan." Stopping, he stared off into space, his thoughts distracting him.

"But how could you do it?" Bella pressed, needing to know. Needing to understand. "How could you torture them? Us? Over and over again?"

Now he moved, but she stood her ground as he came

closer. Tipping her head back so that she could look into his eyes.

"Ah, Bella. My darling Pet." The tone of his voice was gentle, almost tender, as he cupped her chin in his hand, stroking his thumb over her cheek. "Don't look for ulterior motives that you'll be able to understand or mistake me for a good man. I'm not. I did what I thought to get what Earth needed. What I needed Earth to have, for myself to prosper... I did what I did to get what I wanted." He leaned down, his lips brushing over hers for just a moment as he held her immobile. She almost whimpered when his lips moved past so that he could whisper in her ear. "And because I liked it."

Then he released her, leaving her trembling, aroused, furious, and he was walking out of the door.

"Goodbye, Pet."

The words echoed in the room that was now empty except for her.

———

She never told Alex about the Wolf's last visit. There was no point in angering him even more. They left the next day, on a giant ship filled with colonists. Ned was Captaining. When they reached their destination, Alex would take over as leader, Ned continuing as his right-hand man. The men had managed to make up their differences over the past few months, and Bella was relieved by it. She had chosen to take charge of human relations, especially between the citizens of the Moon and Earth. Her team would be essential, throughout the long trip and once they arrived, to keeping the peace and sustaining morale.

Everyone would have to work hard when they made planetfall. But everyone was prepared for that. Those from the Moon were determined to never be in the same situation again, those from Earth were thrilled for a new start. Both sides were surprisingly amicable as they got to know each other over the long trip.

Sometimes, when they were in the quiet and privacy of their own room, Alex would tie her down to the bed, with her ass in the air, clamps on her nipples, and spank her until her ass was bright red. His cock would throb in its ring, til neither of them could take it anymore. Then he'd fuck her until they were both screaming out their orgasms, lost somewhere between reality and fantasy, the present and the past, and the desires that they'd discovered.

And sometimes, back on Earth, a man would stand outside... and stare at the stars.

THE END

BUT WAIT...THERE'S MORE!

The Warlord's Captive Duet is now complete!

But the story isn't over yet. Did you enjoy Jordan and Trish? Their book is next! Make sure you dive into Captain's Captive with Taken and Claimed.

Grab yours today - https://books2read.com/taken-sa

LOOKING FOR MORE FROM SINISTRE?

Check out Butt Stuff, a collection of 8 short stories by Sinistre Ange!

It's not the end until she gets it in the end.

In the world of smut, there is one act still considered so taboo, so forbidden, only a few authors dare to even mention it.

Join Sinistre Ange on the dark side, as she takes you through tale after tale of naughty girls getting it in the tail. From a Christmas Eve Surprise to a special kind of Party Game, these stories are only for the most daring reader.

Because sometimes, the wrong hole... is oh so right.

Dive into your copy today!
http://www.books2read.com/buttstuff

ABOUT SINISTRE ANGE

Sinister Ange is a *USA Today* best-selling author and the alternate pen name for Golden Angel. She is happily married, old enough to know better but still too young to care, and a big fan of happily-ever-afters, strong heroes and heroines, and sizzling chemistry.

She believes the world is a better place when there's a little magic in it.

www.sinistreange.com

ABOUT GOLDEN ANGEL

Golden Angel is a USA Today best-selling author of heart and bottom warming romance.

She is happily married, old enough to know better but still too young to care, and a big fan of happily-ever-afters, strong heroes and heroines, and sizzling chemistry.

When she's not writing, she can often be found on the couch reading, in front of her sewing machine making a new cosplay, hanging out with her friends, or wandering the Maryland Renaissance Fair.

www.goldenangelromance.com

BB bookbub.com/authors/golden-angel

g goodreads.com/goldeniangel

f facebook.com/GoldenAngelAuthor

instagram.com/goldeniangel

After years of working in different aspects of the publishing industry, Niki Roge and Rayanna Jamison came together to form Get That Book Publishing, known as GTB Publishing. GTB Publishing is a small press publishing house with a focus on anthologies and indie authors.

Within GTB Publishing, we have designed 4 specific publishing brands for readers and authors alike to easily find the tropes and books that fit them best.

GTB Publishing focuses on dark romance. From gray to pitch black, dark romance lovers everywhere are going to find something to satisfy their desires.

Dirty Daddies Publishing focuses on Daddy Dom, age play, DDlg, and all aspects of Daddy romance. This brand was established in 2018 and has many USA Today and bestselling anthologies already and is now being expanded to accept Daddy books of all kinds!

Passionate Pages Publishing focuses on all aspects of romance that doesn't fit into the above categories. From contemporary to sci-fi to everything in between, you'll find something passionate in the pages!

Red Hot Romance focuses on newer authors, shorter stories, high spice and lots of power exchange!

Find more information about us:

Website: https://gtbpublishing.com/

Newsletter: https://gtbpublishing.com/newsletter/

Facebook: https://www.facebook.com/gtbpublishing